Twenty-Four Potential Children of Prophecy

Emily Martha Sorensen

Also by Emily Martha Sorensen

Books:

Black Magic Academy
The Keeper and the Rulership
The Fires of the Rulership
Worlds of Wonder
Tabby, Tabby, Burning Bright
Trials of a Teenage Werevulture

Fairy Senses:

Fairy Eyeglasses
Fairy Compass
Fairy Earmuffs
Fairy Barometer
Fairy Pox
Fairy Slippers
Fairy Lunchbox

Dragon Eggs:

Dragon's Egg
Dragon's Hope
Dragon's First Christmas

Comics:

A Magical Roommate
To Prevent World Peace

To Ben and Wednesday,

because doing homework with Wednesday
gave me this story idea,
and Ben was nice enough to let me help her.

CHAPTER 1

ONE DAY IN THE MARKET, WHEN THINGS GOT RIDICULOUS

It was Prophecy Day at the market, and I had to duck through and dodge around hundreds of people as I fought to get to the front of the crowd. The food stalls around the edges were selling snacks and breakfasts in a frenzy, and the whole place had the air of a festival.

"Watch it!" a one-legged former soldier shouted at me as I shoved past him.

"Sorry — well, sorry-ish!" I shouted back, elbowing somebody else out of the way.

Before last month, Prophecy Day had been a boring routine. The prophecies were always correct, but they weren't usually interesting. Who cared about how many puppies the king's hunting dog would bear the next week? Who cared that it would rain the next day? Who cared what color the king's daughter-in-law would wear to tea with a foreign ambassador?

Wait, that was a bad example. She'd screamed and thrown a public fit right there in the marketplace, which the crowd had found highly entertaining. According to the rumors, she had later tried to flout the prophecy by wearing the blue dress she had originally planned on, but the moment she had arrived at the party, a juice-bearing servant had tripped and launched a barrel of bright red juice up into the air, and it had poured all over her with a sticky splash.

Every thread of her blue dress had been dyed in the exact purple hue the Fates had predicted.

You never messed with the Fates. Their prophecies always came true.

So yeah, there was the occasional entertainment, but there had been no real incentive to come to the market just in case the king's family provided a spectacle. Every soothsayer in the entire kingdom spoke the same prophecy, so all you needed to do was pass one on a street corner and blithely ignore their annoyed looks or their unsubtle hints asking for money.

But then last month, the prophecy had been that the king would perform a "great act of generosity." I'd been close enough to see the wild-eyed horror in the king's eyes, and then he'd rapidly reached into his purse and started throwing coins out into the audience. There had been a mad scramble, a giant uproar, and now practically the entire population was trying to cram into the marketplace just in case the Fates made him do it again.

I tried to shove past a bony middle-aged woman and her short-haired daughter, and then I discovered it was my mother and sister.

"Do you mind?" Ma snapped.

"Lemme through," I said. "I'm the one who caught the coin last month."

"Which is why it's one of your siblings' turns!"

"Pshaw," I snorted. "I'm the one most likely to catch a second one."

"But you didn't share it with the rest of us!" she fumed.

"It was *money*," I said. "I didn't want to share it."

"You never want to contribute to society!" Ma snapped. "Here you are, twenty-one, still living at home —"

"— because I'm Pa's apprentice in fixing stuff —"

"— not earning your own money —"

"— because Pa's too cheap to pay me —"

"— doing nothing but rooting through garbage all day —"

"— because rooting through rich people's garbage to find stuff to fix and sell is my job —"

"— instead of getting married, like you should be!"

Veiet groaned. My short-haired little sister was rather sick of this argument. I wasn't. I enjoyed fighting with people. I usually won.

Ma enjoyed fighting, too. The two of us were well-matched. My oldest brother used to roll his eyes whenever he saw one of us open our mouth when the other entered the room, which happened a lot because we both liked to talk. That'd been before he'd gone off to war and gotten killed.

"There's no 'should' about getting married," I shot back. "If I don't want to, I don't have to. There's no legal obligation."

"But you ought to!" Ma said. "You could save some young man's life that way!"

"Only if I started having kids right away," I said. "Don't wanna."

Ma gaped at me in horror, even though I'd said this hundreds of times. The thing was, if a man was over eighteen and married and had at least one child under the age of two, he was ineligible to be drafted. If he'd had six children or more, no matter what their ages, he was permanently excused.

King Wilheld, the current king's pa, had instituted that policy when he'd noticed that the population had been going into critical decline, probably because murdering one percent of the population every year in a senseless war that hadn't ended in half a century was a really stupid idea. Rather than oh, say, instituting peace talks, he'd decided to make sure the population restored itself.

It'd had an immediate and positive effect on the population growth, so much so that his son, King Derroll, had been able to increase the annual number of men and boys drafted twenty years later. I supposed I should've been grateful that that law had been passed, given that I probably wouldn't have existed without it, being the sixth of eight kids, but meh. The war just needed to end already. None of us common people *cared* about the gold mine on the border between both kingdoms that both kings wanted. And we really, really didn't care about which king's grandpa had betrayed whose during the last war a century ago.

Ma was still talking, and I processed every word while my mind whirred over more interesting matters. I interrupted when I heard a good opening.

"— is a civic duty for a young woman to restore the population, and refusing to consider it is selfish —" she was saying.

"Nope, not selfish," I said. "It's very generous."

"How do you figure that?!" she demanded.

"There aren't enough men to go 'round," I said. "Unless the law changes to allow bigamy, I'm being very generous to make sure other young women have the opportunity to marry and make babies."

"Oh, what generosity," Ma said acidly.

Veiet put her hands over her ears and glared at both of us.

A trumpet sounded far ahead of us, signaling the arrival of Crown Prince Kierkin on the castle balcony.

People craned their necks upwards to look, and urchin cutpurses darted through the crowd, doing good business thanks to the distraction. One of them darted near me, and I shifted my weight to display what looked like a stuffed purse hanging down from my belt. It was actually a decoy, since I always kept my real purse tucked into a hidden pocket under my armpit.

An urchin darted in to slice the strap and snatch the decoy.

"Gotcha!" I cried, spinning around seizing his hand. I grabbed the knife away as the urchin wriggled and shouted. "Hey, Ma, want a knife?" I asked, tossing it to her.

"Nah," Ma said, catching it. "Wouldn't hold a decent edge. It's so blunt, I'm shocked he's been able to use it at all."

"Get off! Get off!" the urchin shouted.

"'Kay, listen up, kid," I said, switching arms as he tried to sink his filthy teeth into my left hand. "You want a free meal and a chance at some honest work?"

"Leggo! Leggo!" the kid screamed.

"Come to Fourth and Broad after sundown," I said. "It's the house at the end with a boot on the door."

"Leggo! Leggo!" he screamed.

I let go, and the urchin burst free. He launched himself out into the crowd, dodging between people until he'd disappeared. He didn't even try to seize his knife back.

"He probably won't show up," Veiet said.

"You never know," I shrugged. "About half of them do."

"And less than half of those take you up on it," Ma grumbled. "The freeloaders're eating us outta house and home. And none of them ever bathe. And most of them never say thank you, either!"

"Still worth it," I said. "Best scavengers in the city. And least conspicuous. We're lucky that nobody else is hiring them yet."

"There's a reason for that," Ma muttered.

"Okay, nobody else but the crime lords who get mad unless we pay them a share of the profits to make up for stealing their employees who are secretly stealing stuff from us anyway," I amended.

"*Right,*" Ma said. "We used to have a normal business before Dar made you his apprentice!"

"Yeah, normal in the sense that we were always broke and never had enough to eat," I shot back.

"At least we didn't have to worry about stuff being stolen out of our home!" she hissed. "And most of the extra profits go to feeding those scamps in the first place!"

I was about to add that crooked little scamps had every bit as much a right to eat as we did, which was a touchy subject with Ma and would no doubt have sparked another gigantic argument, but the trumpets sounded again, more loudly, signaling the arrival of King Derroll at the castle balcony hanging above the marketplace. I glanced up to see him standing with his fists clenched, looking like he was dreading a repeat of the very same event that everyone else here was hoping for. I grinned.

The crowd surged forward to get closer to the spot directly under the balcony, and I was separated from Veiet and Ma. That was fine; I'd see them later. I was pretty sure I saw my brother Orran off to the left, but I made no attempt to meet up with him, either. Much as I wanted to catch any money that rained down myself, the next best thing would be if one of my siblings did it, so it was best if we were all spread throughout the crowd anyway.

Somebody beat a loud, thundering drum solo, and hundreds of soothsayers and fortune tellers stood up from their perches along the edges of the crowd, where they had been waiting. The king's own personal soothsayer and fortune teller appeared from behind him and stood on each side of the balcony.

Prophecy Day was about to begin.

CHAPTER 2

TWO PEOPLE I JUST PLAIN DON'T LIKE AT ALL

Lightning lashed down from the clear sky to strike the top spire of the castle, and then it did it again. The Fates had a penchant for spectacle.

And then all of the people in the city who could see the future, or had at least claimed they could, spoke up in unison. None of them stood near me, but there were so many voices speaking, it was like a tide that washed over me, impossible to miss or ignore.

"The days of the war are numbered. The one who will end it now stands within this square. You will know her by the mark of the star she bears on her hand. She will rule the kingdom with wisdom and grace."

The tide of the voices instantly ceased, and was replaced by a gradual hubbub that swelled to enormous volume. Everyone was shouting and looking at each other, grabbing strangers' hands or yelling excitedly.

"The war will be over," I murmured, stunned. "The war will be over. I don't believe it."

There would be no more biannual draft. No more fearing for my brothers' lives, or my neighbors', or my cousins'. I'd never thought much about the Fates before, but now, if I could have kissed them, I would have.

I looked up at the king to see how he was reacting, and he looked speechless with horror. The crown prince had gone purple-faced. It took me nearly a second to realize the obvious, the reason why.

"'She will rule the kingdom with wisdom and grace,'" I murmured.

It might not just be the war's days that were numbered. The king had no daughters, so there were no female heirs who might be given the throne from his line. The Fates might have also just pronounced an end to his family's authority.

My skin tingled with excitement. The king versus the Fates . . . it was like something you saw in a play. There had been whispers of revolution for years. Was it going to happen?

"What will he do?" I wondered. "Will he try to fight the prophecy? He has to know he would lose. Or will he do the intelligent thing, and try to find a way to twist it to achieve his own ends?"

"Silence!" the king bellowed from the balcony. "Silence!"

Nothing could stop the crowd from humming with excitement, or the fervid volume that was rising higher and higher.

King Derroll made a gesture, and more voices were now shouting with him from around the edges of the square. Most likely the guards he always kept stationed around during Prophecy Day.

"SILENCE! SILENCE!"

The crowd gradually calmed down slightly, or at least the noise faded to a dull murmur that the king's shout carried over.

"No one will leave this square!" he bellowed. "No one will leave the marketplace without being checked out by one of my guards! The one who will end the war is standing right here, and the Fates mean us to find her. We will find her today!"

The crowd roared in agreement.

"We will find her, and she will end the war!" the king shouted.

The crowd roared in agreement.

"She will lead us to victory!" the king screamed.

The crowd roared in agreement.

"If you see any girl or young woman who bears the mark of a star, you will bring her to my guards!" the king bellowed. "The sooner this child of prophecy is identified, the sooner she can lead us to victory and finally end the war!"

The crowd's roar drowned out all thought and rationality. I had to plug my ears with my fingers, and it still drilled into my brain with the force of a thousand headaches.

"Good job," I approved. "He just interpreted the prophecy for the Fates, adding several assumptions that weren't stated in the prophecy at all. By doing so, he's made it easier for the prophecy to be fulfilled by working with him, rather than against him. His insistence on victory bothers me, though, since that implies extra deaths. What's wrong with a peace treaty?"

The crowd continued to shout around me.

"His insistence that 'she' is a child is amusing, though," I said. "A child would be less of a threat to his crown in the immediate future, and there's always the hope that he might marry her off to his second or third son. He's managed to completely miss another ambiguity that he might have exploited, of course. The prophecy said 'the kingdom,' not specifically stating Horhold, which meant it could be stretched to interpret it to mean some other kingdom — such as Gemina, our enemy. He should have figured that out and declared that 'she' would rule Gemina after we conquered it."

My voice was drowned out as the noise swelled louder because of the discovery of a four-year-old girl with a star-shaped birthmark on her wrist. A woman who was probably her mother screamed as the child was yanked away.

The king's face glowed. "We have found —"

"Here!" someone shouted.

"We found her!" somebody else cried.

There was confusion and even more shouting and screaming as more girls or young women were thrust towards the guards. Four shoved their own hands in the air and yelled for the guards, eagerly volunteering themselves. Chaos reigned, and the king started to look more and more frenzied.

"What's this?" someone screamed hysterically, pointing at me. My palms had been facing outward while I'd stuffed my fingers in my ears. "We've found another one! I've found one! It's her!"

"What?" I asked, stunned. "No, you're wrong. See —"

"See the mark?" that person screamed, grabbing my arm and waving my right hand above the crowd. "See the mark? See it?"

"That's not a birthmark, it's just a burn that I got last month!" I shouted.

But in no time, I was caught and herded over to the others, who stood huddled in terror or confusion or smugness. Three of them were little girls who ranged from four to six. One wore the robes of a fortune teller and looked vaguely superior. Two wore rich finery.

"I always knew the Fates meant me for something grand," one of the young women in a sumptuous gown pronounced.

"What's going on?" a scared girl who looked about ten asked.

The four-year-old was crying.

"The Fates have decreed that we will all be witnesses to history, even if we do not make it," the fortune teller intoned.

"The Fates have decreed that there will be a female person with a mark of a star on her hand who will end the war and rule the kingdom with wisdom and grace," I snapped. "That's it! This is completely ridiculous!"

The fortune teller smiled mysteriously. "Those who ridicule the will of the Fates will be even more bound to it."

"I'm not ridiculing the will of the Fates!" I said indignantly. "I'm perfectly fine with somebody being the so-called 'child of prophecy,' I just know it's not me."

"Denying the will of the Fates only ends in tragedy," she said, shaking her head.

"I — I don't want to be here," one of the rich girls stammered. "I just want to go home. I'm not supposed to be part of the war!"

"No need to worry," the other rich girl said loftily. "Once they realize it's me, all the rest of you will be released, and I'll receive my rightful authority."

"Ruling the kingdom?" I snorted. "Yeah, I noticed that, too. You might be able to convince the king to whore you out to one of his sons, but there's no way you're the one in the prophecy. That star on your hand was clearly drawn on with ink."

The rich brat sneered and pulled a sleeve over her hand that held the smeared black mark, as others craned to look at it.

"How could you be so vulgar?" the other rich girl squeaked. "That was completely uncalled for!"

"You have a point, but I'm not very good at controlling my mouth, and she irked me," I shrugged.

"Well, it's clearly not *you* in the prophecy," the rich brat spat at me. "It's clear you have no wisdom or grace. Do you know who I am?"

"A snooty charlatan who's decided to compensate for her own ugliness by wearing so much jewelry, it makes her look gaudy," I said promptly.

"I am Anna Khordoa! The king's *niece!*"

"Oh," I said. "That explains why you think you have a right to the throne. You're right, you might have a chance of hijacking the prophecy."

"Then apologize," she glowered. "Apologize to me, your future queen."

"I apologize," I said. "I was ruder than I should have been. I should have only been moderately rude, instead of extremely."

"I don't like you at all!" the king's niece shouted. "When I take the throne, punishing you will be my top priority!"

"Right. Sabotaging you it is, then," I said.

"Attempting to sabotage what the Fates have decreed is a sure path to failure and misery," the fortune teller declared vaguely.

"Then *you* be the child of prophecy," I snorted.

The fortune teller spread her hands wide. "If that is what the Fates decree, accepting it would be the path of wisdom and grace."

I looked over at her for a long moment. "I don't like you, either," I decided.

CHAPTER 3

THREE SILVER COINS
THAT SMELL LIKE FEET

King Derroll did not look pleased when we were herded into the castle and brought before him.

"Twenty-four is just too many," he complained. "How are we supposed to know which one the prophecy was referring to?"

"It's me, dear uncle," the rich brat called, raising her hand to show off the ink-smeared mark she had obviously drawn on herself. "All these commoners are clearly irrelevant!"

The king drummed his fingers on the throne he was sitting on. It was made out of polished goldwood, the most expensive wood you could buy, and also the softest. It was said to be useful for the seats of chairs because it would eventually mold itself to your body, but using it for an entire throne seemed excessive. Also —

"You should really not drum your fingers like that," I called from the middle of the pack of girls. "The armrest's dented already. Oh, wait, is that because that's a bad habit you do a lot?"

The king stopped drumming his fingers. "Who said that?" he snapped.

"Me, Your Majesty," I said, waving. "I'm Henina. I'm not the one in the prophecy. Your niece isn't either, by the way. She drew the star on her hand herself."

"I did not!" Anna Khordoa shouted, hiding the incriminating evidence under her sleeve.

The king drummed his fingers on the throne again.

"I told you, you shouldn't do that," I said. "Or you shouldn't have had the armrests made from goldwood in the first place if you have that habit. That was poor planning on your part."

"Silence!" he bellowed.

"I'm not really good at silence," I said.

"Stop! Talking!"

"I'm not really good at that, either," I said.

The king rose to his feet, and many of the young women and girls around me cowered. Anna Khordoa shot me a triumphant look.

"Looking smug doesn't make you more attractive," I told her.

"What we have here," the king said loudly, talking over top of me, "is a problem. With just one child of prophecy, our path would be clear. She would have to be trained in the arts of warfare, put in charge of the army, and sent to the battlefield."

"Excuse me, isn't that illegal?" I asked. "Women aren't eligible for the draft."

"But twenty-four potentials complicates things," he went on, standing imposingly. The fingers on his right hand twitched, and he clenched his jaw and stopped them. "I have no way of knowing which one of you needs to be trained."

"Or you could send the child of prophecy as an ambassador instead," I said. "Hold peace talks and just plain stop fighting. Or we could surrender with the condition that Gemina doesn't get to invade. The kingdom's spent far more on the war than it would have gained from those gold mines in the first place, so it'd really be the sensible thing to do."

"Silence!" the king roared.

"I told you, I'm not good at that," I shot back. "And even if I were, I wouldn't want to be right now. There's an obvious solution if you can just get past your ego."

One of the guards stepped forward, drawing his sword from his scabbard. He stared at the king meaningfully, as if to say that the only thing holding him back was an order.

I swallowed. The threat was clear. I didn't think he'd actually run me through or anything, but maybe I should make the attempt to stop scolding the king. I bit my hand to keep from talking.

There was a moment of silence, itchy silence, which I was dying to fill with something. So I bit down harder on my hand. Ow ow ow.

"So," the king said at last, putting his hands on his hips and glaring down at each one of us in turn, "the only path we can take now is to train and educate all of you. From now on, you will all live in the castle, and not one of you will be allowed to leave for any reason."

Gasps rang through the crowd, and the four-year-old girl burst into tears. The six-year-old looked around in confusion, saw the younger girl crying, and then started howling with her.

"That's not fair!" the ten-year-old girl shouted.

The guard raised his sword arm, which he'd let droop, slightly. The ten-year-old screamed and ran behind one of the young women, cowering. A few of the others in the crowd whimpered, and I looked behind me to see angry expressions growing on other faces. Off to the side, Anna Khordoa looked exultant, and the fortune teller looked unbothered.

I opened my mouth to demand why she seemed so perfectly okay with this, but I felt my hand on my teeth and remembered. Right. I was trying not to talk. I hated not talking. It reminded me of when Ma used to make me stand in the corner until I could keep my mouth shut, which never worked, because when I was mad or scared or noticed something interesting, I needed to say something, and right now I was all three —

"Who puts a cushion on a goldwood chair?" I burst out, unable to stop myself. "Why would you do that? The whole point of goldwood is that it doesn't need cushioning!"

The king turned around and stared at me incredulously.

"And also you have a loose thread on your sleeve," I said, "and that guard over there is probably being bribed, and Anna Khordoa's not the only one who put the mark on herself because that one right there was looking horribly regretful —"

"Bribed?" the king roared. "What makes you say that?"

I blinked. I thought he'd be more interested in the fact that there were two potentials who could be eliminated. "It's just a supposition," I said, "but he's got three silver in his right shoe. It clinked as we were walking in."

"That's not silver!" the guard I'd pointed at shouted from across the room. He wasn't the one who had brandished the sword, but he was one of the ones who had marched us into the castle, so I didn't feel particularly bad for telling on him. "They're coppers!"

"I know the sound of irons, coppers, and tins, and it wasn't any of those," I shot back. "I suppose it could have been golds, since I'm even less familiar with those, but I don't think anyone would bribe a guard with enough money to buy a house. Unless Gemina paid him to assassinate the king or something," I added thoughtfully. "I suppose then it could have been golds —"

"Remove your shoe!" the king shouted.

The guard stood there, frozen.

"Remove your shoe," the king said in a dangerous voice, "or I'll send you to the front lines with no weapon to act as a shield for somebody else."

"I-it was just draft dodge money," the guard stammered, pulling off his shoe. "Everyone does it —"

"Remove your shoe!" the king bellowed.

The guard's shoe popped off, and three silver coins went rolling across the floor. In a flash, Anna Khordoa leaned over and snatched one.

"Congratulations, you now have a coin that smells like foot," I told her.

"I don't know what you're talking about," she sniffed.

"I've met honester cutpurses than you."

The king ignored the trifle of an entire month's worth of pay having been snatched up by his niece, and he scooped up the other two silvers from the floor. "Don't do it again," he grunted.

I waited for him to say the guard was fired, but he didn't. The guard just put his shoe back on and straightened, looking humiliated, and he shot me an angry glance.

"Wait, is that it?" I asked, outraged. "He accepted a bribe! He let someone out of the draft! That's illegal! You should at least find out what names he's agreed to remove in the past so that you can reinstate them! If rich families can just get out of the draft —"

Anna Khordoa snorted contemptuously.

". . . then they won't protest the war," I finished flatly.

The king ignored me, turning to the guards beside us, including the one who had admitted to accepting the bribe.

"Take them to the servants' quarters," he said, waving his hand at most of us. "Anna and Asaya can each have a guest room."

The two rich girls were separated from the rest of us, one of them whimpering softly and the other smirking, and a guard escorted them both out of a doorway in the back. The rest of us were taken through a side door and down a steep, narrow flight of stairs.

We passed a kitchen with steam and heat billowing out of the doorway, filled with scullery maids and shouting cooks. We passed a pregnant maid scrubbing soiled sheets against a washboard.

"Four people to a room," one of the guards said, while another opened a door.

I wrinkled my nose. "That room is tiny. And it's covered in dust. It's clearly only meant for two or maximum three people. The dust makes sense if it's been empty, but the least you could do is clean it if we're going to be guests —"

"You're not guests," the guard I had embarrassed snapped. "You're prisoners. Four to a room."

And that was how I wound up being crowded in with a little girl, a young woman who seemed scared of me, and the fortune teller, who blithely volunteered to join us in the first room.

CHAPTER 4

FOUR'S A CROWD, AND SO IS SEVEN

Complaining didn't seem like it would help much, but I did it anyway, more out of habit than anything.

This had the unintended consequence of driving two of my roommates out into the hallway, begging for sanctuary in the sixth room at the end of the hall. The two young women there, who apparently had taken a strong dislike to me, volunteered to let them stay in their room instead.

So that worked out surprisingly well.

"Ma always said being annoying doesn't get you anything, but I don't know what she was talking about," I grinned.

The fortune teller, who had elected to stay, said nothing.

"You gonna vacate the room, too?" I hinted.

"No," she said.

"I'll really get on your nerves," I said. "People are so touchy."

"There are six bedrooms and twenty-two people," she said mildly. "You are not going to get your own room."

I pouted a little. I'd never had my own room, seeing as I'd always shared with at least two of my sisters, so it would have been a nice novelty. At least I wouldn't have to share with the king's bratty niece, but the fortune teller was almost as bad.

I flopped onto my bed, which was a mistake because it was hard and cold and narrow and I banged my hip against the wall.

"Ow," I complained. "This bed is cold and hard and narrow and I banged my hip against the wall."

"When one chooses an unwise path, one must accept the consequences of one's unwise choices," the fortune teller said mildly.

"Yeah, I really don't like you," I said, looking over at her. She had seated herself neatly on her skinny bed and was watching me with creepy intensity. "It's like you're being vague on purpose. Not to mention preachy. And you're looking at me with creepy intensity."

She smiled.

"That smile implies that you're being deliberately vague and preachy and you're trying to look at me with creepy intensity," I told her.

The smile vanished. "It is not always necessary to speak."

"I don't really have a brain-mouth filter," I explained. "I just sort of think things and they come out."

"That," she said, "will not serve you well."

"People always say that, but I've done fine so far," I grinned.

She looked deeply displeased.

"Are you going to move to another room?" I asked hopefully.

"No," she said.

I flopped back down on my bed.

"Ow," I complained. "This bed is cold and hard and narrow and I banged my hip against the wall again."

"One might say that those who cannot learn from their mistakes are destined to repeat them," she murmured.

Before I could reply, which I was about to do, a knock sounded on our door.

Startled, I jumped up and opened it. Standing in the hallway was a fat, balding man wearing a toga.

"You're the king's soothsayer, right?" I asked. "I'm not sure because most soothsayers are fat and old and balding, but your toga looks new and your sandals aren't dirty, which means you weren't outside an hour ago, unless you washed them of course."

The man's expression went sour. "I am the king's soothsayer."

"What are you here for?" I asked. "Are you eliminating the false children of prophecy? If so, you'll want to start with Anna Khordoa, then move on to the young woman with black hair in ringlets —"

"No," the soothsayer cut me off. "I am here to speak to all of you regarding your duties and responsibilities. Come."

He left the doorway, and we heard a knock at the door next to ours. I hopped out of my bed, which was a mistake because the floor was hard and uneven and I tripped and banged my hip against the wall in the exact same place.

"Ow," I complained. "The floor's hard and uneven and I tripped and banged my hip against the wall in the exact same place."

"That is the Fates' way of informing you that you should not keep trying to eliminate potentials," the fortune teller informed me.

"I'm going to ignore you now," I told her.

The soothsayer gathered us all into the hallway, and then he led us back towards the kitchens in a rapid pace. This time, we walked right through the room filled with heat and steam, with cooks shouting and dishes clattering, and what looked like a sumptuous feast being laid out on carts.

"I'm hungry," I announced loudly.

No one said anything.

"Is this food for us?" I called.

"No!" the soothsayer shouted from ahead of us, his voice barely audible over the noise.

I was uncomfortably pinned in by seven people crowded against me, which was way too many, so I slid to the back of the crowd, with only one other person on each side of me.

We passed by a cart with an array of fancy cakes, so I grabbed one and stuffed it in my mouth. It was amazing, all light and fluffy and melty. I chewed and swallowed rapturously.

"You should try one of those cakes," I nudged the young women on either sides of me. "They're amazing."

They both gave me horrified looks.

"Here comes another cart," I told them. "That looks like roast duck. You get the duck, you get the boiled roots, and I'll grab the rolls and preserves. Ready . . . set . . ."

The cart rolled by, and I snatched five rolls and one saucer of preserves off the cart as the exhausted-looking scullery maid trudged past, her eyes drooping. The duck and boiled roots, sadly, remained in place.

"It's like you two aren't even trying," I remonstrated. "You need to take lessons from a pickpocket someday."

One of them looked horrified. The other looked embarrassed.

I dipped one of the rolls into the preserves and took a huge bite. It was delicious, but I was starting to feel a bit lightheaded from all the fluffy stuff with nothing solid to go with it.

"Here," I said to each of them, handing over a roll and holding out the saucer. "We can't all have useful acquaintances. Sorry I didn't think about that."

One of the young women held the roll, looking unsure of herself. The other reached for the saucer hesitantly.

"What are you doing?!" a cook screamed, spying us. "Are you stealing food? You no-good, dishonest thieves!"

One of the young women threw her roll to the ground as if stung, and the other one just stood there, frozen, while the cook marched over and snatched the roll from her and the dish of preserves from me. The cook seized the one on the floor, ran to dump both rolls and the dish of preserves back onto the cart, and scolded the scullery maid loudly.

One of the young women beside me burst into tears. The other one glared at me.

"You're not putting that roll on the king's table after it's been on the floor, are you?" I called to the cook.

Her eyes blazed and she said nothing. She looked like she might spit fire in rage.

"Yeah, good point, what's good enough for commoners is good enough for the king," I said, nodding.

She stormed over to the cart, seized the two rolls she had dumped back into the bowl, and flung them across the room. They landed in the fire underneath a bubbling pot that was giving off most of the heat and the steam.

"Good aim, but that's a real waste of food," I said. "You could at least have saved those for the king's dogs."

The cook looked about to snap, but then the pot started to bubble and boil over, so she shouted and shoved scullery maids aside to stir it.

"Thief," one of the young women beside me hissed.

"No, but I've watched them," I said. "It's very educational."

Another cart rolled by, this one with a very alert-looking pregnant woman pushing it, so I didn't try to convince the untalented two to snatch food; I just whipped my hand out and grabbed a stack of several slices of meat, secreting them up my sleeve. The meat felt slimy and clammy, and I could hardly wait to eat it, but the corner of my eye informed me that the cook off to the side was watching us suspiciously again.

We reached the end of the kitchen and exited it. I slid my hand up my sleeve and tried to tell by feel how many slices I'd grabbed.

"Four, maybe?" I said out loud. "I could give one to each of the kids, but that would only leave one for me, and they might be even worse at hiding it . . ." The noise of the kitchen no longer masked my talking.

The soothsayer stopped and spun around. "What was that?!"

"Nothing," I said immediately.

"She stole food!" one of the young women next to my cried.

"And she got us in trouble for it!" the other one exclaimed.

"And she's still got two rolls up her sleeves!" the first one added.

The soothsayer marched over and held out his hand.

Grumpily, because I had been planning to save the rolls for later, I wriggled them out of my sleeves while carefully keeping the folds of meat at my right elbow. The extra weight at my elbow was obvious, but then again, other people didn't always seem to notice things that seemed dead obvious to me, and this soothsayer was no exception. He just took the rolls, stuffed them into his toga, and marched back through the crowd to the front to lead us again.

"Having no brain-mouth filter is really inconvenient," I said.

The young woman at my elbow sniffed and pointedly ignored me.

"More for me, anyway," I shrugged, shaking the meat slices into my hand and shoving them into my mouth in one smooth movement. I chewed extremely quickly and gulped so fast that the large-ish chunks got stuck in my throat. I swallowed with difficulty to make them go down. I really needed water.

"Can I get some water?" I called. "I feel like I'm choking. I chewed too fast and swallowed the meat too quickly."

The soothsayer froze and turned around, staring at me.

"When's dinner?" I added. "I'm still hungry."

CHAPTER 5

FIVE MINUTES LATER, WHEN MY PATIENCE SNAPPED

Given the way the soothsayer snarled at me and waved his arms while giving some kind of lecture that I could have recited every word back from but otherwise paid no attention to, I was pleasantly surprised when there was food laid out on the table in the room he guided us to.

"I love it when there are no consequences for my poor behavior," I grinned at one of the young women as I helped myself to stale bread and lukewarm water that was brownish because it didn't seem to have been filtered very well.

She glared at me and said nothing.

"Okay, fine, maybe a few consequences," I amended, pouring some of the sediment-laden water into a cracked cup. "You don't have to dislike me. I've got nothing against you. You made no impression on me at all, actually."

She stormed off and flopped down on a cushion. Somebody had thoughtfully brought twenty-five cushions into the room, and most of the others had already taken one to sit on.

"Well, not that thoughtfully," I said out loud. "Most of the cushions are threadbare, all of them are stained, three of them have stuffing coming out, and five of them smell. I don't know if they've ever been washed. It's clear that this is not a room where important people meet, and that's a little inconsiderate given that one of us is a child of prophecy."

The door opened behind us, and the two rich girls were brought in. Anna Khordoa stared at the cushions with a pinched look on her face, and she shuddered when she saw the water.

"For once we're in agreement," I said, nodding.

"Sit," the soothsayer said, waving his hands, "and we will discuss the opportunities before you all, and your responsibilities."

Most of the other girls obediently grabbed a final few hunks of stale bread and poured themselves a final glass of murky water before taking a seat on one of the cushions strewn around the room. Two of the children dipped their bread into their water to soften it. Anna Khordoa did none of those things. She stood, with her arms folded.

I sniffed my cushion, which smelled like unwashed dog. The places where the stuffing was coming out might have been bitten or clawed.

"We're sitting on the king's dogs' chew toys," I told everyone around me. "It's nice to know how much respect he has for us."

"Your position," the soothsayer said, raising his voice, "is one of great uncertainty, but great importance. In this, I do not speak of just the one among you who will ultimately fulfill the prophecy, but of all twenty-four of you. Indeed, we might say that all twenty-four of you are one-twenty-fourth a child of prophecy."

Young women sat up straight, pride rising in their eyes. Small girls' eyes glowed.

"That's stupid!" I said loudly. "One of us is a child of prophecy. The other twenty-three are not. You can't just redefine the term to mean whatever you want it to mean."

The smile slipped from the soothsayer's face. Hostile glares shot at me from around the room.

"Every one of you is special —" the soothsayer began.

"No, one of us is special, and twenty-three of us are going to go back to our normal lives after this involuntary captivity, preferably with some delusion that it all served some grand patriotic purpose so that it doesn't seem completely pointless, just like the war." I stopped to take a breath.

"The Fates' wills are mysterious!" the soothsayer all but snarled. "It may be that they wished to have you all here for some purpose, and that the end of the war will necessitate all of you —"

"Then why didn't the prophecy mention twenty-four of us?" I asked.

"— with perhaps only one being obvious, yet all of your contributions being equally essential and valuable —"

"I still don't feel like my question's been satisfactorily answered."

Anna Khordoa let out a choked laugh.

Amidst fuming, the soothsayer explained to us that we were to be educated in basic warfare skills, as well as tactics and strategy.

"No diplomacy?" I asked. "Come on, it's obvious there's at least one person here who could use lessons on that." I pointed at myself.

Anna Khordoa snickered again.

"You will be expected," the soothsayer said self-importantly, "to read at least one book on tactics or strategy every week, as well as to attend lessons on self-defense, swordplay, and archery —"

One young woman tentatively spoke up. "Um . . . I can't read."

"Me, neither," said another one, sounding relieved.

"Or me."

"Or me."

"Or me."

The soothsayer looked very aback. "Can *any* of you read?"

"I can," Anna Khordoa said self-importantly.

"And me," the other rich girl ventured, looking nervous.

"I pestered the bookbinder down the street until he taught me the basics, and I figured out the rest by myself," I volunteered. "Ma loved it because it kept me away from the house for hours at a time. I tried to teach my siblings, but they didn't see the point because nobody owns books except rich people."

"I can read cards, but not books," the fortune teller said in a low voice.

Nobody else spoke up.

I looked around, amazed. "Is that it? Just the three of us? Really? Okay, everyone else needs to learn right away. Don't worry, I picked it up in just a few months. It's easy."

The soothsayer looked taken aback. "I don't think —"

"I learned on a philosophical treatise the scribe who worked for the bookbinder was illustrating," I said. "Do you have one of those around? It must have been good for beginners because it worked well for me."

Most of them stared at me blankly. Anna Khordoa's eyes grew big, and the quiet rich girl looked kind of ill.

"Oh, if you don't have that exact one, I can recreate it," I said. "Give me a bunch of paper and a pen and ink and stuff, and I'll write it down. It'll take a few days and it'll be really boring, but if it'll help, I'll do it. Just don't make me do it twenty-one times. If you need separate copies for all the beginners, make the king's scribes do it. I'm not so good at drawing, so I can't redo the illustrations, but —"

"Hang on," Anna Khordoa interrupted. "Are you saying you could rewrite the whole thing, word for word, *from memory?*"

"Yeah . . .?" I said slowly. "Why is that surprising? I read it several times when I was a kid. I didn't understand all the words, and there are some I still don't get, but —"

"I want proof of that," the soothsayer snapped. "You *will* be required to write the whole thing, and to not have any contact with anyone else until you've finished."

"Oh, come on!" I exploded. "Is this my punishment for being nice? Look, I'll write you out the first page right now — is that sufficient? Get me a piece of paper and ink and stuff right now!"

The soothsayer stood and walked out into the hallway. He returned a moment later. "There is someone fetching those things," he said gravely.

A man who looked like a scribe, with ink on his fingers and nose where he had probably scratched it, opened the door and wandered in with a roll of paper, a glass pen, and a pot of ink. He started to walk toward the soothsayer, then gave an angry shout as I popped up from my cushion and grabbed them.

"Don't worry, they're mine," I said promptly, flopping down across the floor and swinging my crossed legs in the air as I opened the ink pot. "He wants me to prove something. I don't know what his problem is, but I was just trying to help and now he seems to think I was lying. By the way, the food in here was awful. The bread was stale, and I tasted mold. That's not exactly going to motivate me to not steal stuff from the kitchen."

"Don't talk, *write,*" the soothsayer snapped.

"I can do both," I said, carefully forming the letters as I moved through the second line. "Reading is fast, but writing is ponderous. I haven't really practiced it much. Only when we've found leftover stuff for it in rich people's trash, and that doesn't happen much."

"Trash . . .?" the scribe said, sounding taken aback.

"That's what we do. We find people's trash and we fix it and sell it," I said. "Pa just used to fix stuff, but he wasn't making enough money, and then I found out lots of people grab stuff from rich people's trash and try to use it even if it's broken, so then I thought we could make way more money if we did both, which is true except that it's way more competitive, so we have to pay kids to help us, usually in food that they eat right there because then nobody can take it from them, which means really we aren't making as much profit as we should be, but —"

"I'm sure you could write much faster if you didn't talk," the soothsayer interrupted. "You're only on the third line right now!"

"I'm sure you can't make me stop talking," I responded, "and I'm going as fast as I can. By the way, this is a word I don't know. What's 'sibylline'?"

The scribe glanced down and yelped. "That's Aristhene's treatise on the qualities of the Fates! Why is she writing that?"

"To prove I've read it, because apparently that matters, which seems kind of dumb to me, but he insisted —"

"Is that what she's writing?" the soothsayer yelped. He scrambled over and snatched the paper away from me. "This is not something a commoner should have read! This is a beginners' lesson for soothsayers!"

"It's not like there's anything in it that's not in the plays," I said. "The narrators pontificate without end."

The soothsayer clenched his jaw.

"Do you want me to write the rest?" I asked shrewdly. "I'm hoping you'll say no because it's really boring, but if you want me to write more and show it to everybody —"

"Definitely do not write any more!" he shouted. "You have proven your point!"

I grinned.

The fortune teller watched me very solemnly.

CHAPTER 6

SIX BORING BOOKS
TO READ WHILE TALKING

Our schedules were drawn up without our input or permission. Most of the older girls and young women were assigned to have lessons in tactics and strategy read aloud to them, while the youngest three were to be taught in the same things by a separate tutor who would explain things at a much simpler level.

"You really think the four-year-old is going to become a tactical genius after just a few lessons?" I asked the younger girls' tutor skeptically when he came in to introduce himself. "Okay, but their time would be better spent learning useless things that rich girls do, just in case they need to be married off to one of the king's sons later. It'd be pretty disgusting if the four-year-old were married off to the sixteen-year-old, but hey, if the king's paternal grandparents did that, I somehow doubt he'd hesitate to —"

"Quiet!" the soothsayer said sharply.

"I wasn't talking very loudly," I said.

The younger girls' tutor looked kind of dazed.

The three of us who could read were excused from the lessons, and each handed a stack of six books instead.

"You'll be required to finish all those by the end of the week, and to report on what you've learned from each one," the soothsayer informed us. "If you cannot do so, you will be sent to join the others."

"What if we'd prefer to learn in that way in the first place?" Anna Khordoa asked haughtily.

"Your life might depend on how much you learn," the soothsayer said darkly. "I suggest you apply yourself."

The quiet rich girl clutched her books nervously.

The other twenty-one were marched away to their destinations, while the three of us were locked into this room to do nothing but read. I, of course, kept up a steady commentary.

"This author's really fond of the word 'verily,'" I said. "He wrote it three times in the first paragraph. Oh, look, another one. Oh, look, a fifth. Hey, do either of you know what this word means?"

I got up and wandered across the room to show each of them the page.

"We're supposed to read, not talk," the king's niece said through clenched teeth.

"I can do both," I said, flipping the page. "It's a good thing, because I think I've been reading more slowly than both of you. I must have had less practice."

"We're not going to get *any* reading done if you keep *talking!*" Anna Khordoa snapped.

"That would definitely make me look more impressive," I said, my eyes darting down to the next line. "If I've read a whole lot more than you have, I mean. It's already referencing stuff I'd never heard of, but I guess I can just parrot back what it said when I'm asked what I've learned later."

The other girl put down her book and closed it. "My name's Asaya," she said. "What's yours?"

"Henina," I said. "How'd you get your star mark?"

"Birthmark," she said, holding her left arm out.

"That's not on your hand," I noted. "It's not even on your wrist. It's halfway up your arm. It doesn't even look like a star. It looks more like a wart or something."

"I know," she said, "but I got brought here anyway."

"And now you're stuck," I nodded. "And if that's not on your hand, the prophecy definitely doesn't apply to you. Think your parents might get you out of this?"

"I hope so," she sighed, "but my father's the king's third cousin. I'd be ideal to marry off to one of the princes. I suppose I wouldn't mind too much, but going off to war, that sounds . . ."

"I'd rather die than marry either of the princes," Anna Khordoa said loftily.

"You mean because they're your first cousins?" I asked.

"No," she said with annoyance. "That's perfectly legal, and in fact common when arranging a political alliance. I mean because the crown prince is married, which means the other two are just leftovers."

"Good point," I said. "If the prophecy actually applied to you, as opposed to you having put the mark on your hand yourself, which by the way is now smudged so much that it looks like a bruise, you wouldn't have to worry about that because you'd be fated to rule. But since it doesn't, you couldn't just count on the crown prince suddenly dying or something. Unless you hired an assassin, I suppose."

"I would never do such a thing," Anna Khordoa said, though her eyes brightened.

"Your eyes brightened," I said. "I'll tell the king you're planning to assassinate one of his sons."

Her eyes darkened. "Don't you dare. If you try it, I'll —"

"I'm not sure why you think threats would stop me from blurting it out the first time I think about it while he's around," I said.

She glowered. "Fine. I promise I won't. If you do blurt it out, tell him I said that after *you* suggested it in the first place!"

I shrugged. "I can't really predict what I might say."

"Um," Asaya said nervously, raising her finger to get our attention, "if you want to rule Horhold, wouldn't marrying either of the princes be better than not, Anna?"

Anna Khordoa looked over at her and smiled. "The prophecy didn't say that one of us would rule Horhold. It said that one of us would *rule*. And a conquered nation would be ripe for a change in government."

"Oh, you noticed that, too," I said.

"Of course I did." She smiled. "Why do you think I dr— discovered this miraculous mark placed on my hand by the Fates, and declared myself the most likely candidate?"

"The Fates sure draw messily," I said.

"Because I knew Gemina would be in dire need of leadership," Anna Khordoa said grandly. "And the Fates mean me to be the one to do it."

"If by 'the Fates' you mean 'whatever writing implement you had in your pocket at the time,' then I would agree."

"And my dear, dear uncle will no doubt be delighted by that fulfillment of the prophecy," she went on, "because it will be in his best interest as well as my family's."

"Yes, he does seem like a selfish pig," I agreed. "Why did you have a pen in your pocket, anyway?"

"If I had, it would only have been because it was the Fates' will that it be there," Anna Khordoa announced.

"Yes, I'm sure it was the Fates' will, because they love fakes."

"You're so naive," Anna Khordoa sighed. "Most of the soothsayers and almost all of the fortune tellers in the kingdom have no power to see the future, they just claim they have. The Fates don't *care* about fakes. They treat the charlatans exactly the same as the real ones."

"I find that deeply unsettling," I said. "My stomach's churning. That might just be because of the stale bread I ate, though, because I think there was mold on it."

"That's servants' fare," Anna Khordoa said smugly. "Don't expect it to get any better. We get to sup in our rooms, so the food's superb."

"In that case, I'll save my moldy crusts and hide them on the king's plate later," I said.

"You'll just get the cooks in trouble," Asaya said.

"Okay, I'll do it and take credit for it," I corrected.

"Have you no sense of self-preservation?" Anna Khordoa demanded. "You seem to be trying to offend all the most influential people around you!"

"Not true," I defended. "I haven't said anything rude about Asaya, even though she looks like a mouse and her voice squeaks like one, too."

Asaya gasped, putting her hands to her mouth. Her eyes filled with tears.

"I'm not sure whether to be amazed or appalled," Anna Khordoa muttered.

"Try both," I said, and flipped the page of my book.

"Don't ignore me!" Anna Khordoa flared.

"I'm not ignoring you," I said. "I've been glancing down at the page this whole time. I don't know what a trebuchet is. Do you?"

The door made a noise, and we all turned to look. The lock scraped open, and the king's soothsayer stood there with the key in his hand.

"It just occurred to me," he said, "that perhaps I should separate you three if I want any reading to get accomplished. Should I?"

"*Yes!*" Anna Khordoa and Asaya both shouted.

"I can read just fine while talking," I said.

The soothsayer had an I-knew-it look on his face.

"You look like you're thinking, 'I knew it!'" I commented.

"Yesss," he said slowly. "My powers of prediction are vast, but this didn't require them."

"Are you a real soothsayer or a fake one, like Anna Khordoa says most of them are?" I asked interestedly.

"And that brings it up to four influential people that I know of you've offended today," Anna Khordoa muttered under her breath.

CHAPTER 7

SEVEN INFLUENTIAL PEOPLE I'VE OFFENDED TODAY

After an hour of reading in my room, I got bored and decided to get up and wander around.

I took the book with me just in case I found a task that was both entertaining and easy to read while doing, such as stoneboard. No one had managed to beat me in that game in years. Maybe somebody in the castle would stand a chance to try.

"They really should have installed locks on our doors if they didn't want us wandering around," I said cheerfully, shutting the door to my room. "Oh, I know, maybe they have another spare room like the ones Asaya and Anna Khordoa are sleeping in. I could sneak into one of those tonight so I don't have to sleep two feet away from the fortune teller."

I suddenly realized I was speaking aloud, and made a conscious effort to stop.

"This is just like the way Ma says she always knew when I was about to get in trouble because I'd narrate exactly what I was doing," I muttered. "Which way should I go? The end of the hall is a dead end, and if I go through the kitchen, that cook will be watching for me. She recognized me and shook her fist when I was marched through the kitchen back to my room. Okay, up the stairs to the throne room it is."

I ran to the stairs and hurried up them.

"I really hope the king won't be there," I murmured. "Anna Khordoa had a point about offending influential people. I just didn't know how *not* to."

Well, maybe the whole being-a-potential-child-of-prophecy thing would help prevent my head ending up on a chopping block. Not that I believed for a second that I was the real one. I didn't have a personality that could stop wars. I'd be more likely to start them.

"Of course, the prophecy didn't say anything about whether the war would end and then immediately be replaced by another one," I said out loud. "The days of that particular war *could* be numbered if I picked a fight between both kingdoms and a much bigger neighbor, such as the Erghan Empire. Then they'd have to team up in order to both survive. Maybe I shouldn't mention that to anybody."

I reached the top of the stairs, and luckily, nobody was in the throne room, not even a guard. Unluckily, when I tried all the doors, they were locked.

"Okay, fine, I'll read here," I said. "That goldwood chair looks more comfortable than my lumpy bed, anyway."

I moved over to the throne and sat on it, wriggling around.

"Yeah, this doesn't conform to my backside," I decided. "His Majesty must have an immense bottom."

I heard rattling from one of the doors, and I jumped up, panicked. I looked around for somewhere to hide, started to run for the stairs, and then heard footsteps coming up those. I dove behind the throne.

"I'm just asking if you can predict which one's the real one," the king's voice said, and a door opened from the wall opposite the staircase I'd come up. "Why is this too much to ask? You two can see the future, can't you?"

I yelped softly and stuffed my fist in my mouth. I could do this. I could stay silent so nobody noticed me. I could definitely do this. I would read my book while I was listening in. I didn't usually read out loud, because the scribe had hit me over the head with an ink pot every time I'd done it in front of him, and that'd broken me of the habit. Where was the book I was supposed to be reading?

I checked my hands, my pockets, and the floor around me. I didn't have it. I'd apparently dropped it someplace. Perfect.

"It's not that simple, sire," a woman's voice said. "The stones and cards agree with everything the prophecy said, but the *who* is ambiguous."

"And the stars?" the king snarled.

"It's barely past lunchtime, sire," the soothsayer said soothingly. "The stars won't be out for hours. I'll be able to read them then. I'm sure I'll have a much more accurate prediction from them than 'the *who* is ambiguous.'"

"I didn't say there were no indications at all," the fortune teller said hastily. "There were three who stood out as especially likely candidates. The cards said that you yourself, King Derroll, will have recognized them as the best choices before anyone."

"Well," King Derroll said thoughtfully, "I did wonder about Anna."

"The one blessed by the Fates that the cards predicted!" the king's fortune teller cried. "She had the cards for fortune and power beside her."

"And one of them had the robes of a fortune teller," the king said. "Like yours, only shabby. I wondered if the Fates would take more notice of her, being what she was."

"The Fates do, indeed, highly favor those with our gifts," the king's fortune teller said mysteriously. "Her cards indicated a blessing from the Fates, as well."

The king's soothsayer snorted derisively.

"I can't really think of a third one that stood out," the king added, sounding puzzled.

"Think," the soothsayer said in a confident tone. "I'm sure one will spring to your memory. One who made a large impression on you. Perhaps . . . perhaps she had some unusual beauty . . .?"

"Oh!" the king said. "That one! It didn't even occur to me, but of course she'd be one of them. Sorran, what was the name of that one again? The one with the golden hair?"

"Laell," the soothsayer's voice said, "but if you ask me, I'm surprised the one who made the biggest impression on you wasn't the one who wouldn't stop talking. Even her name means 'henpecked.'"

"It does not!" I shouted from behind the throne. "It means 'child of hens'!"

"Get out from there!" the king's voice roared.

Reluctantly, I stood up.

"What if the world," the soothsayer said, looking weary, "were you doing back there?"

"Looking for a place to read that was more comfortable, except I seem to have dropped my book — oh, there it is," I said, hopping over the throne and scooping it up from the seat. "You're all pretty unobservant, aren't you?"

The king's face was rapidly turning red.

"If you ask me," the soothsayer said, "I think she's one of the three most likely. I'll have to read the stars, of course, to be sure, but she seems exactly like the type the Fates might pick."

"Then the Fates are stupid," I said, "because I'd be a terrible choice."

There was an aghast silence.

"Did you just insult the *Fates?*" the fortune teller yelped.

"Amazing," the soothsayer muttered under his breath. Louder, he said, "You realize you just pretty much invited them to torment you now."

"I didn't do it on purpose," I said. "Anyway, they probably weren't paying attention."

Something rumbled outside, and I glanced to the side just in time to see lightning flash from a clear sky and hit a bird flying past the window. Feathers flew everywhere.

"That doesn't mean anything," I said.

An identical bird flew past, going the opposite direction. Lightning flashed again and hit it. Feathers flew everywhere.

"Okay, maybe that does," I said.

"It seems you have the Fates' attention," the soothsayer said dryly.

"Maybe not all three," I said. "Maybe it's just one of them."

Three birds flew past the window, and three bolts of lightning flashed from the clear sky to hit them. Feathers flew like a flurry of black snow.

"Or maybe it's all three," I said.

"I think," the king said, with a rather gleeful expression on his face, "that I will leave your punishment for insouciance to the Fates. I'm sure they'll do a better job of punishing you than I possibly could."

"Yeah, that's pretty worrying," I agreed.

"*Why?*" the fortune teller burst out, incredulity overwhelming the mysterious air she'd seemed to be trying to project. "Why would you insult the Fates?!"

I glanced at the soothsayer. "Still think I might be the person in the prophecy? The one with wisdom and grace?"

"Hmmmmm," he said. "I'm strongly reconsidering."

EIGHT MINOR ISSUES I SHOULD REALLY HAVE CONSIDERED

Even though a punishment from the king wasn't forthcoming, I didn't feel like I'd gotten away with anything without consequences, and that worried me. I'd seen plays. I knew I didn't want to be a target of the Fates.

So when I was escorted back to my room with orders to not leave unless I *wanted* consequences, I flipped through the pages of the various books, not even trying to learn anything, just looking at the pages so that I could try to figure out the contents later if anyone asked me.

About two hours later or so, I heard a chatter of conversation moving down the hallway, and then the door squeaked horribly as it opened. Noise surged past behind the fortune teller as she entered our room, her face still and solemn.

"Are you a fake fortune teller or a real one?" I asked her.

She said nothing, merely walking to the thin bed on her side of the room.

"I'm thinking the king's fortune teller is a fake one," I said. "Perhaps the soothsayer is, too. And if you were real, you wouldn't have gone to the market and wound up here."

"No one can predict the Fates' prophecies," the fortune teller said, not turning around to look at me. "Their prophecies are never fixed within the future until they are spoken."

"In other words, you're a fake," I said. "The Fates control fate. Everything they do must be predestined."

"No," she said, "the Fates are outside of fate. They do everything by the capriciousness of their whims."

She still wasn't turning around to look at me. It was really annoying.

"You're still not turning around to look at me," I said. "It's really annoying."

She turned slowly, and her eyes looked thoughtful and mysterious. She said nothing.

"Are you seeing the future right now?" I asked curiously. "If so, what am I going to eat for lunch when they feed us?"

"If I tell you, you might change it," she said in a low voice. "That's the way the Fates work. They can see the future, and thus they can change it."

"They could do that anyway," I said. "They control fate."

"No," she said, "they don't control fate. They control —"

A burst of laughter came from the room next to us, drowning out her last word.

"They control —" she began again.

Another burst of laughter drowned her last word out.

"They control —"

Several voices shouted from the room next door, and then another burst of laughter rang out.

"It is clear they do not want you to know," she said.

"Maybe it's because I offended them earlier," I said, considering.

Her mouth fell open. "You . . . offended the Fates?"

"Yes, if you could really see the future, you'd have known that already."

"Perhaps if I had read your cards, I would have," she said slowly.

"The soothsayer thinks I might be the child-not-that-I'm-a-child-at-all of prophecy that the Fates intended," I said.

She nodded solemnly. "Your abilities and unusual education level for your class strongly imply that. Your weaknesses are also consistent with what the Fates would find entertaining. If you wish to accept that fate, all you should need to do is relax and let them drive that future forward."

"What if I *don't* want to accept that fate?" I asked.

She surveyed me. "Why would you not want to?"

"Because the prophecy doesn't say how peace will happen or how long it will last, and I'm more likely to start a war than stop one," I said promptly.

"Not if you rule with wisdom and grace," she said.

My face twisted. "And let them change my entire personality? That would be just as bad. Well, just as bad for me. Probably better for everyone else in the world, really."

"The Fates don't have the power to do that in any case," she said. "They only control —"

A burst of laughter came from the room next door.

"— coincidence," she finished as soon as the laughter had stopped. A rumble of angry thunder came from outside.

"Yes, yes, we know you're mad about it," I said loudly.

"You might perhaps consider not deliberately taunting the Fates," the fortune teller said, her eyebrows twitching.

"That's not taunting," I said. "Taunting would be saying, 'What are they going to do? They can't just kill me if they want me for something!' Oh, but I suppose they could kill my family or something."

The fortune teller's eyebrows twitched more vigorously. "*Wisdom* would be not saying any of that. It might also involve reminding them that they will have far more entertainment from you if you are alive and have not learned to be cautious about what you say."

"True," I agreed. "I probably would be a lot more cautious or at least afraid to talk at all if they did something drastic like killing my family. It would definitely stop me from taking them lightly again."

The fortune teller looked very alarmed now. "But it's precisely that irreverence that makes you so potentially entertaining. Any reverence you learned for the Fates would also translate over to powerful humans, such as the king."

"No, not really," I said.

"Are you *trying* to convince the Fates to make your life a living hell?!" she exploded.

"No," I said. "I'm just really, really bad at shutting my mouth."

"Unimaginably bad," she muttered.

"No, it's perfectly imaginable," I said. "What if I wanted to make you the child of prophecy? What would that take?"

She sighed. "Unfortunately, I do not believe that path is viable any longer."

"Why not?" I demanded. "You're a fortune teller, right? You have the Fates' attention. And the mark on your hand is a scar, not just something you drew on."

"You are to blame," she said, and a faint hint of annoyance rose in her voice. "Your insistence on eliminating some of the potentials has caused speculation to run rampant among the other girls. Most of them wish to fulfill the prophecy themselves, and the rest wish for the suspense to end as soon as possible. Thus, they are all looking for excuses to eliminate each other."

"And they found a reason to eliminate you?" I asked.

"One of them noticed me run into the market square after the prophecy had been spoken," she said resentfully. "Under normal circumstances, this would not have been a problem, because the Fates do not care about truth, only about what seems to be. But since you have insisted on there being *one* true child of prophecy, and not a smorgasbord of options for the Fates to choose from, everyone is seeking for holes in the others' stories. Anyone who is believed to be inconsistent with the prophecy has had their chances punctured."

"So you, Anna Khordoa, the girl with the ringlets who also drew her mark on herself . . ."

". . . and Ena, Heila, Terrina, Aival, and Dureen," she finished. "Eight in all. Eight opportunities for the Fates to choose somebody other than you that are now all dashed to pieces."

I winced. "Eight minor issues I should really have considered. Okay, how do we fix this?"

"Fix this?" The fortune teller looked incredulous. "There is no way to fix this. There are now only sixteen potentials remaining, and that number will decrease every day. By having segregated yourself apart from the rest, you've greatly decreased your chances of their finding a hole in your story, and greatly increased your chances of being the one they all believe is real. The more who believe it is you, the easier it will be for the Fates to make that true."

"So what you're saying," I said, "is that I need to interact with the rest so they'll find reasons to eliminate me."

"That's not what I said."

"That seems simple enough," I nodded. "I just need to make sure you never go anywhere without me again."

"That's not what I said!"

"Don't worry," I assured her. "I won't make any specific plans. I'll just improvise. That way the Fates won't know how to thwart me."

"Maybe if you learned how to not speak your plans aloud," she said in quiet indignation, "you would be able to make better plans than following me."

"And yet, there it is." I grinned. "Don't worry. I'm pretty good at stoneboard. And that's *despite* the fact that I can't plan far ahead without telling the opponents my strategy."

CHAPTER 9

NINE EAGER HANDS THAT WANT A HANDOUT

Morning dawned, and the soothsayer came to collect my roommate. The outside of our door jiggled as he unlocked it.

"Somebody installed a lock on our door last night," I announced as the door opened. "It was really loud and it woke me up. Was it because I snuck into the throne room yesterday and would totally do it again if I could?"

He turned a deaf ear to me. "Come, Helga," he said briefly.

The fortune teller stood up from her thin, lumpy bed.

"You're trying to ignore me so that I won't get on your nerves," I said. "That's what my older siblings do, especially the ones who are married. My oldest sister got really mad when I asked why she wasn't pregnant again yet, since her second child had just turned two and I assumed she wanted her husband to be ineligible for the draft again."

The soothsayer's eyebrows twitched, and he turned to herd the fortune teller out of the room.

"Oh, by the way, you can have these back," I said, popping up from my bed and grabbing the stack of books from beside me. "I can't read them anymore."

He stopped and glanced at me. "You're done already?"

"No, I can't read them anymore," I said. "I can't read. I completely forgot how."

He stared at me incredulously.

I grinned.

"That's impossible!" he exploded.

"Easy come, easy go," I said loftily. "I learned to read so quickly, why shouldn't it disappear just as quickly? Memory like a sieve, that's me."

"You quoted an entire treatise from memory yesterday!" he shouted.

"Memory like a very *inconsistent* sieve," I explained.

"Or a very convenient one," he muttered. Louder, he added, "I can see what you're trying to do, and the answer is no. You will not be leaving this room. You will stay here all day reading."

"That's too bad, because I can't read anymore, so I'll just have to figure out a way to pick the lock instead," I said. "I've never done it before, but a few of my acquaintances have told me how they do it, and it doesn't sound very hard."

"You'd have nothing to pick it *with*," he snapped.

I shrugged. "The bed frames are made of unlacquered sliverwood, so it should be easy to yank off a few dozen long, hard pieces and get to work. By the way, I can't believe you give your servants furniture made out of unlacquered sliverwood. It might be incredibly cheap, but it's also inhospitable and downright crass. The least you could do was have somebody lacquer it."

"I'll post a guard outside your door," he said, glaring at me. "If you even so much as try to pick that lock —"

"Do I look like a person with impulse control?" I asked. "You don't want somebody to accidentally kill me. The Fates might get cross about that."

The soothsayer stared at me for a long moment, his expression heavy. The fortune teller looked from one of us to the other, her expression unreadably blank.

"Do you think your ability to read might come *back* tomorrow if I send you to study with the other girls today?" he demanded.

"You never know, but it might at least keep me out of trouble today," I said promptly.

He looked extremely annoyed. "Fine. I suppose that's not too much to ask. You'll be easier to keep an eye on that way anyway."

"I'm easy to keep an eye on," I said. "As long as by 'eye' you mean 'ear.'"

He grumpily escorted us both out of the room and down the hallway, then through the kitchen and down a flight of stairs in the opposite direction as the meeting room we'd gone to the day before.

The cooks watched me so closely as we walked through the kitchen that the fortune teller surreptitiously slipped nearly half a bowl of fruit and several shreds of meat into her billowing robes. I was so impressed with her skill that I nearly mentioned it several times, but the soothsayer kept shouting "Shh!" with evident annoyance.

He delivered us to a room with nine other potentials breakfasting on moldy bread, and then left. There was no lock on the door.

"Did you bring us food?" the six-year-old girl cried, dropping her moldy crust and racing over.

The fortune teller opened her robes and handed the child a dried drait and two squished yellowberries, which had leaked and left the inside of her robes all sticky. She didn't seem to have noticed.

"Thank you!" the little girl squealed.

"Can I have some, too?" the ten-year-old girl begged.

"And me?" a young woman who looked about fourteen pleaded.

"And me?" added the one with the curly black ringlets.

The fortune teller nodded, and walked around to hand a few morsels to everybody.

"You shouldn't steal food," a young woman glared as she was handed two yellowberries. She was one of the ones I'd gotten in trouble yesterday. "What'll you do if they find out?"

The fortune teller shrugged and made as if to take the berries back.

The young woman quickly snatched them back and popped them in her mouth.

"I'm really very impressed with your skill," I announced as she walked past me and went to the next person. "Even if you just skipped over me. That was rude. I've seen pickpockets who could learn from you."

"How do you think I survived as a child?" the fortune teller asked.

"Now I feel sorry for you," I said. "Maybe I should call you your name. The soothsayer called you Helga. Should I stop calling you 'the fortune teller'?"

"What you call me makes no difference to me," she said, handing a dried drait to the last young woman who was holding out her hand for a share. "That name is not a real one."

"Why not?" I demanded. "Do you have some reason to hide your name? Are you somebody famous in disguise?"

"No," the fortune teller said shortly. "I simply don't remember it."

"Oh. Now I feel *really* sorry for you," I said.

"I prefer not to be pitied," she snapped.

"Too late," I announced. "By the way, why didn't you share the meat you grabbed, just the fruit?"

Nine eager hands shot out.

"I ate it on the way here," the fortune teller said tightly.

"That's so selfish!" one of the young women shouted.

"You'd better get us some for lunch," the one I'd gotten in trouble said huffily.

The fortune teller looked grumpy.

"I don't think she agrees," I said. "I bet she's thinking you're all being selfish. Which you are. Learn to say thank you or something. You're as bad as the cutpurses my ma feeds!"

Offended looks appeared all over the room.

"What are you doing?" the fortune teller asked me.

"I'm helping you," I said.

"Stop helping."

"Okay," I said. I wandered over to the door.

"What are you doing?" she demanded.

"The door's not locked," I explained. "I don't feel like interacting with the rest when they come. I've had enough for one day."

"Do not sneak off," she said stiffly. "You will get us all in trouble."

I grinned. "You mean that's not the course of wisdom and grace?"

The fortune teller developed a trepidatious look on her face.

"Bye now!" I said cheerfully, pulling on the door handle and slipping out of the room.

In the hallway, I ran into two of the other potentials who were sleepily trudging towards the room for breakfast. I saw them coming and veered towards them so that I deliberately crashed into them.

"Ow!" one of them complained, holding her head.

"Oops," I said. "That wasn't very graceful of me."

"You did that on purpose!" the other girl accused.

"If I did, it was a terribly unwise thing to do," I said, shaking my head. Then, because I couldn't stop myself, I added, "Hint hint."

They both stared at me blankly.

"Right, I'm off to go unwisely wandering the castle and ungracefully bumping into people," I said. "I'm terribly clumsy, as you can tell. So very graceless. I don't suppose we're going to take dancing lessons where I can show off just how bad I'm going to be?"

One of the young women still looked blank. Realization dawned in the other one's face.

"Are you trying to pretend you're not the child of prophecy?" she accused me.

"No, I'm showing everyone why I'm not," I said cheerfully. "And you should definitely play along with it, seeing as the wart on your hand is definitely star-shaped, you were one of the first to get discovered, and one of your relatives was killed in the war so you have every reason to want to stop it."

Her mouth fell open. "How did you know that?"

"I guessed," I said. "Most people know someone. Who was yours?"

"My uncle," she said in a low voice.

"My older brother," I nodded. "You?" I asked the other girl.

"A boy I liked," she said sadly.

"Right." I clapped a hand on each of their shoulders. "The war needs to be stopped, and either one of you could be the one to do it. I'm rooting for both of you. Also, don't ask the fortune teller for stolen food because she didn't steal enough for everybody, and don't tell her you feel sorry for her, because I think it'll just annoy her."

Both young women looked shocked and baffled.

I waved and turned the corner away from the kitchen, hoping to explore where I hadn't been before, and I completely coincidentally ran into the king's fortune teller.

CHAPTER 10

TEN IMPOSSIBLE THINGS FOR BREAKFAST

Whoops," I said immediately, turning around. "I meant to go in that direction."

The woman reached out and seized my wrist. "We must speak."

"I was hoping you wouldn't notice I was trying to get away with something," I complained.

She pulled me closer, and hissed, "The charlatan who claims he can read the stars believes that you are the one chosen by the Fates. The cards show me you wish to prove this is not the case."

"Or you were just listening in on my conversation with the others ten seconds ago," I said.

She released my wrist. "His false predictions must be ended. Do you wish to have my aid?"

I eyed her. "You're both fakes. You just want to prove the other wrong so that the king will only listen to you."

"Believe what you wish," she intoned. "It is of no consequence to me. Do you wish for my aid?"

I shrugged. "Sure, if it'll actually help. But it'll be confusing if I think of my roommate as 'the fortune teller' and you as 'the king's fortune teller,' so unless you can think of something better, I'll think of you as 'the self-important charlatan' from now on."

"Then come with me," the self-important charlatan said, turning in a way that made her robes swish out dramatically behind her.

"Nice dramatic effect," I said, following her. "I always thought fortune teller robes were supposed to be humble and self-effacing, but you've managed to turn humility into a form of grandeur. How much did it cost to have the patched and ragged places perfectly stitched?"

"The king provides," the woman said in a vague voice, "and I wear only what he considers appropriate. I personally have such poverty that cost holds no meaning for me."

"No, that's called being rich," I said. "Poverty-stricken people are obsessed with money."

She continued down the hall silently. Her robes billowed artfully.

"You realize fortune teller robes always billow in plays because it implies that they're ill-fitting," I commented. "Because fortune tellers are so poor that they barely eat. Yours were made with extra fabric, and the weave is a complicated one that makes even scratchy fibers soft and comfortable. I've watched one of the spinners on our street make cloth with that weave, and it takes ten times longer than normal and three times as much thread. I bet your clothing cost as much as an average ballgown."

The self-important charlatan woman pushed open a door. "We have arrived. I shall read what your stones have to say about you."

I followed her into the room, which was lit only by flickering candlelight because the windows had been blocked by heavy curtains. The candles were a well-crafted variety, and they didn't fill the room with the odor of rancid, burning pig fat. There were elaborate cloth charts hanging all around the walls of the room.

"Yep, nothing unusual about this setup," I said. "Most fortune tellers just draw charts in the dirt."

She seated me in a chair next to the table in the middle of the room. She unhooked three of the charts from the wall and flung them across the table in a practiced motion, then smoothed out the wrinkles as she made sure they overlapped in some pattern that made no sense to me. Then she reached under the table and pulled out a large, lidded box. She removed the lid, and it was filled to the brim with precious stones. They twinkled in the dim candlelight, all different shapes and sizes. It was a very impressive sight.

"Can I keep some of those?" I asked hopefully. "That would be the best kind of aid."

"These are not for selling," she said coldly. "These are intrinsic tools for my discipline. Their value lies not in their cost."

"I know a few dozen street urchins who would disagree," I said. "Most fortune tellers use pebbles from the road, you realize."

"You must stop comparing me to those less experienced," she said stiffly. "When one's role is to foresee the future of kings, one must have the best tools available."

"When one can impress by results, one doesn't need to impress anyone by their tools," I retorted.

"The right tools are essential to produce the right results," the woman said coldly.

"The right results being 'whatever keeps you in favor with the king,'" I agreed, nodding.

Her cheek twitched. "Do you wish for my aid or not?"

"I don't mind," I said. "I'm certainly not on the soothsayer's side. Do you want me to reach in and drop them?"

"If you would," she said, holding out the box to me.

I reached in, ran my fingers through stones that were worth more than I would ever otherwise hold in a lifetime, and scooped up as many as I could. I let go, and they whumped into the cloth charts. The self-important charlatan grabbed one that looked like a ruby as it nearly bounced off the table.

"Right," she said, leaning forward, examining the reading. "The first thing that the stones say is that you have one of them up your sleeve."

I sighed and removed the amethyst, or perhaps it was a purple sapphire, from up my right sleeve. The fortune teller's hand shot out and grabbed it without looking.

"The second thing," she continued, "is that the Fates' will is not absolutely set on who will fulfill the prophecy."

"Yes, I already know that," I said. "My roommate told me. Amazingly, without amethysts or rubies."

"If you wish to avoid this fate being placed upon your shoulders," the self-important charlatan said, carefully perusing a line of stones, "then three things are needful."

"Not having wisdom, not having grace, and not stopping the war," I said. "Got it."

She swept aside the stones along the edges that had not landed on any of the charts and poured them back into the box. Then her eyes narrowed as she stared at the stones and cloth for a long time.

"I'm starting to get bored, and also that circle is drawn slightly lopsidedly," I said, pointing to a chart. "You should have used a compass, not drawn it freehand on the fabric. Do I need to be here?"

The fortune teller looked up. Her eyelids were slightly lowered, giving her a mysterious air. "The first thing you must do," she said, "is to eat ten impossible things for breakfast."

"Apparently we don't define 'impossible' the same way," I said. "How do you define it?"

"The second," she said, "is to cease offending anyone of import for the rest of the day."

"Oh, *that's* how you define impossible," I said.

"The third —" she went on.

"Isn't two enough?" I asked.

"— is to find somebody else who the Fates will like better for the position."

"I already knew that part," I said. "Is that the best you can do? Giving me two things of nonsense and one thing I knew already?"

She said nothing, starting to sweep the precious stones off the edge of the table and into the box.

My hand lashed out and seized a tiny ruby, and I tossed it into my mouth.

"Hey!" the fortune teller screamed. "What are you doing?!"

"That's my first impossible thing for breakfast," I said. "People would never normally eat rubies."

"Give it back!" she shouted. "The second was to no longer offend anyone today! Have you forgotten so quickly?!"

"But you're not offended," I said. "You're just angry. I'm proving your prophecy right, remember."

She subsided, seeming to be attempting to mask smoldering fury. "Very well," she said quietly. "Go fulfill all three of your tasks, and we will say no more about this."

"Thanks," I beamed, getting up from my chair. "I appreciate the aid."

I left the room and walked briskly down the hallway, checking to see if anybody was watching me. Then I spat the ruby into my hand, tucking it into the hidden pocket underneath my armpit.

"Now to get to Ma and Pa," I said. "I know just what the rest of my breakfast will be."

ELEVEN NASTY SOLDIERS VERSUS THREE LITTLE GIRLS

"Hello!" I said, poking my head into Asaya's room. "I'm glad I finally found you! I wanted to ask you someth— oh, darn, the rich brat's here, too?"

"My name is Anna Khordoa," the rich brat said coldly.

"Yes, I know, but that's how I think of you," I explained. "Because when we first met, that was how you acted. You probably still do, really, I'm just more used to you —"

"Don't think of me that way," she snapped. "Think of me as 'the beautiful king's niece' instead."

"I'll try," I said dubiously. "You're not really beautiful, though."

"What did you want to ask me?" Asaya broke in quickly, probably trying to stop a fight.

"Pretty good peacemaking," I told her. "Maybe you'll be the one to stop the war. Do you know a way out of the castle that I could sneak out of?"

"What's wrong, too scared of the king?" Anna Khordoa mocked.

"No, I got my fortune told and it said that I had to not offend anyone else important today because if I did, I'd wind up the child of prophecy," I said. "I was thinking that the best thing I can do is get away from anyone important. By the way, did I offend you with the 'rich brat' thing?"

"Absolutely not," Anna Khordoa said immediately. "I took it as a compliment."

"How could you take it as a compliment . . .?" Asaya began.

"Just shut your mouth before you say anything about *her*," Anna Khordoa grated, waving her hand at the timid rich girl.

"So, do you know any ways out?" I asked the timid rich girl.

She shook her head quickly, wide-eyed.

"I do," Anna Khordoa said, standing abruptly. The book that had been on her lap tumbled down to the floor. She didn't bother to pick it up or to fix the pages that had gotten creased underneath the weight of the rest of the book. "The sooner we get you out of here, the better. We're going to need the three little girls."

"Okay, but I'd better not offend them," I said. "They're potential children of prophecy. They might be considered important."

"They are not," Anna Khordoa snapped. "From now on, 'important' is defined as only people *I* think are important. You understand?"

"So only yourself?" I asked.

She grinned. "If that's how it has to be."

"In that case, I don't have to leave the castle at all," I said. "I can just hang around you all day, and you can tell anyone I offend that they're not important —"

"Let's get you out of the castle," she said hastily.

After ordering me to stay in Asaya's room, Anna Khordoa swept out into the corridor, shutting the door behind her. She was gone for several minutes, and I picked up the book she'd dropped and carefully folded the pages the opposite way to try to get them uncreased.

"She's not very careful with valuable things, is she?" I noted.

"Anna's one of the most popular and ambitious girls in our set," the timid rich girl said. "You really shouldn't say rude things about her."

"I can say whatever I want about her today," I said. "She can't get offended by any of it."

"B-but she might anyway."

"No, she clearly has more self-control than that," I said.

Asaya was silent for a moment.

"Are you sure this prophecy was legit?" she asked timidly.

"I'm sure it was a prediction, not a prophecy, and I'm almost certain it's not legit," I said. "But what does that matter? If the self-important charlatan can claim she said that, the Fates won't want to go against it."

"The who?" Asaya looked confused.

"That's how I think of the king's fortune teller so that I don't get her mixed up with the fortune teller who's not named Helga."

Asaya looked more confused than ever.

"It's very simple," I said. "The self-important charlatan is really good at looking impressive and making important people believe her. As such, if I fulfill the prediction she made, that'll be seen as strong evidence that I can't possibly be the child of prophecy. If the Fates go against that, some people might think they were wrong."

"But the Fates are never wrong," Asaya protested.

"Exactly!"

She looked confused again.

"It's okay," I said. "If the Fates cared if you understood, they wouldn't have let me explain it to you in the first place. They would have interrupted somehow. That means that you're either not important enough to matter or not smart enough to understand it in any case."

Her eyes filled with tears.

"You're not offended, are you?" I asked worriedly.

She shook her head quickly. "I just — I — I got some dust in my eyes."

"Good," I said with relief. "I hope you'll turn out to be the one who fulfills the prophecy. I bet you'd be good at it."

"Do you think so?" she asked hopefully, sitting up straight.

"Absolutely," I said. "You'd be perfect as a pawn of the Fates."

Her spine sagged and her head drooped.

"I mean, I think you'd be happy that way," I said quickly. "And you'd make a good ruler for the kingdom. And you'd be guaranteed to have wisdom and grace. Those are all good things."

"I'm not offended, so you don't have to make me feel better," she mumbled.

"Do you want to go against the Fates?" I asked her.

"No!" she gasped.

"Do you want a guaranteed fate that will make your life better as well as be good for the kingdom, and keep us at peace forever after?"

She hesitated, and then nodded quickly.

"Then I'll try to make you the child of prophecy," I said.

She swallowed. "But — but Anna wants to —"

"I don't really care what the rich brat wants," I said.

"B-but you said I was ineligible, because —" She pointed to the wart halfway up her arm, which was definitely not a star on her hand.

"I changed my mind," I said, shrugging. "You're a potential, just like the rest of us. And the Fates could always burn or scar you with a star mark if they want to. I just thought of that. The prophecy said nothing about the mark being there that day in the market square. It could just appear in the future on the one they've chosen."

"But then . . ." She seemed to be trying to follow my logic. "But then it could be anyone who was in the market square . . ."

"That's right!" I said cheerfully. "It could be anybody at all! But it's more likely to be one of us twenty-four potentials, because everyone thinks it is. Preferably you, because fewer people will die if it's done diplomatically."

"But Anna —" the timid girl began.

"I don't care what the rich brat wants."

"I told you," a cold voice said from the doorway, "to call me 'the king's beautiful niece.'"

I turned around, and there was the king's beautiful niece standing in the doorway, hands on her hips, her ugly features arranged in an even uglier look of annoyance —

"Nope, doesn't work," I said. "Can I call you 'the king's vain niece' instead?"

"You can call me 'Anna Khordoa,'" she said icily, "and nothing else from now on."

I looked at Anna Khordoa, who had a very offended look on Anna Khordoa's face, even though Anna Khordoa had said that Anna Khordoa wouldn't be offended by anything else I said about Anna Khordoa today, because Anna Khordoa wanted . . .

"Nope, I've gotta at least use pronouns," I said.

She sighed. "Whatever. We've got a limited window of opportunity that's going to open in just a few minutes. Put this on."

She threw a shabby cape at me.

"Where did you get this?" I asked. "Did you steal it from some poor beggar that was standing outside?"

"No," she snapped, "it's the official cape of a draft officer. My uncle is sending out two hundred of them today."

I stared at her, appalled. "Today? We had a draft two months ago! The next one's not supposed to be for four months! And the war's just about to end!"

"That's the point," Anna Khordoa said. "The people are all riled up, which means now's the perfect time to squeeze a few new soldiers out of the city and the towns. Don't you realize he can't afford to be patient? Everyone thinks the war should be ending *now*. He's already preparing carriages to take all twenty-four of us to the battlefront."

I swallowed. The thought that we might be sent there immediately had never occurred to me.

"What are we going to do?" Asaya asked frantically. "I don't want to go to the battlefront!"

"Yes, you do," I snapped, "because you're going to be the one to stop the war. Remember?"

"No, she is not, I am," Anna Khordoa snapped. "In any case, it's even more important to get you out of here if you don't want to be the one to stop the war, Henina. You wear this and you sneak out with the draft officers when the distraction begins. Got it?"

"What distraction?" I asked.

She grinned. "The one I was setting up anyway: eleven nasty soldiers versus three little girls."

CHAPTER 12

TWELVE ATTEMPTS TO OPEN A STUBBORN DOOR

"Uwahhhh!" a little girl's voice screamed from downstairs for the fourth time. "I want my mommyyyy!"

"What exactly did you *do*?" I asked Anna Khordoa.

She shrugged, ripped the cape off my shoulders, tucked my hair down under the back of my shirt, then tied the cape back on again. "I told them if they went downstairs right now, the soldiers would take them back home to their families. I figured they would throw a fit if that turned out to be untrue. Keep your hair tucked in, because if it looks shorter, it won't be as obvious you're female."

The little girl's voice screamed again. "WANT MOMMY!"

"You're a very mean person," I said.

"Don't tell me you wouldn't do the same thing if you needed a distraction," she said. "I wouldn't believe you for a moment."

She headed down the hallway briskly, stood in front of me as several servants rushed past, then went on marching without giving me a single backwards glance.

"That might make it look like we don't know each other, but it isn't very friendly," I remarked. "And I wouldn't say something like that to a child unless I actually meant it, by the way."

"You would if it were the first thing that popped into your head," Anna Khordoa retorted, checking around the corner and glancing back to give me a curt nod. I followed her around it. "Don't try to pretend you're better than me."

"So what do you plan to do if you become queen?" I asked. "Bully more small kids for pleasure?"

"Better than drafting twelve-year-olds to fight in a war, like our current king does," Anna Khordoa snapped. "Just because I've never lost a relative doesn't mean I can't imagine it."

"You have a point," I said.

She stopped at the next corner and checked around it. She held up a finger to shush me.

"Maybe you're not so bad as all that," I continued.

"*Shh!*" she hissed.

"No, never mind, I still don't like you," I added.

"Anna?" A vapidly handsome face topping a very pudgy body appeared from around the corner. "What are you doing out here? Aren't you supposed to be . . . reading or something?"

"Yes," Anna Khordoa said brightly, and I couldn't see her face from behind her, but I was guessing she was smiling in an I-am-definitely-not-suspicious way. I'd tried that before, but it'd never worked for me, perhaps because I always felt the need to add, "I'm not suspicious!" while smiling that way.

"Ah." The dense-looking young man looked perplexed. "Do you need another book to read, or something?"

"Just taking a break!" Anna Khordoa said cheerfully. "Aren't you supposed to be at your swordfighting lesson, Ingram?"

"Oh, that's Ingram, the king's third son!" I cried in recognition. "I knew I'd seen that face somewhere! It looks just like all those masks they use for idiot comic relief characters in the plays. I didn't realize they were all based on him! I should've realized it from the family resemblance to the king's not-beautiful niece!"

Anna Khordoa turned around and shot me a fierce glare.

"Who are you?" the third prince asked, looking confused.

"Nobody," Anna Khordoa said fiercely. "He's nobody. Just a draft officer who's heading out to pick up some more soldiers."

"That's right, I'm one of those cold-blooded scumbags that my older sister always spits at when their backs are turned," I said, nodding.

Anna Khordoa looked like she wanted to pull my hair out.

"Your older sister spits at you?" the prince asked in bafflement.

"That's right. We don't get along."

"Um . . ." The prince seemed to be working backwards. ". . . about what you said about masks . . ."

"The draft officer meant nothing by it!" Anna Khordoa said with a firm, brittle smile. "He was just making a joke that he thought would amuse Your Royal Highness! Ha ha ha! Ha ha ha!"

"Ha ha ha?" The prince laughed uncertainly.

"Now, we must be going," Anna Khordoa said briskly, patting her cousin on the arm. "Lots to do, as I'm sure you know. Enjoy your swordfighting lesson."

"Of course," the third prince said gloomily.

Anna Khordoa whisked me away. As soon as we were safely halfway down a staircase, out of eyesight and earshot, she hissed, "You know, one way to stop you from being the child of prophecy would be to kill you myself."

"You made sure he wasn't offended," I said. "Thanks."

"We're just lucky it wasn't Melkor," she said, glowering. "He's the smart prince."

"Oh, Anna!" a voice called, and a high-cheekboned young man poked his head around the bottom of the staircase. "I thought I heard your voice. Why were you talking about me?"

"She was just saying that I shouldn't offend you," I said.

"Really?" The prince turned his eyes from his cousin over to me. "What are you up to? And why is a woman wearing a draft officer's cape?"

"Funny joke," I said brightly. "Ha ha ha!"

He said nothing.

"Melkor, let me put this in clear terms," Anna Khordoa said. "The Fates are involved. If you don't want to end up forced to marry me, I suggest you walk away and pretend you never saw this."

The second prince opened his mouth, closed it, and then walked away.

"So, you two aren't desperately in love or anything," I noted.

"What was your first clue?" Anna Khordoa asked.

"Mainly the fact that you can't stand each other. It was pretty obvious by the fact that you kept glaring at each other, and he looked dead horrified when you mentioned marriage."

"If only my parents were so perceptive," she snorted.

We reached the bottom of the stairs and headed towards the throne room, where the shouting was coming from. It had grown louder, and I could hear four young women yelling, five men's voices bellowing, and two children weeping.

"Congratulations, you've made children inconsolable," I said. "You must be so proud."

"You'd do the same thing!" she flared.

We walked down the corridor towards the door behind which all the clamor was happening. As we neared it —

A door opened across the hall.

"Oh, Anna!" Crown Prince Kierkin called, holding a pair of sashes, one red and one chartreuse. "I can't remember which one Orry wanted me to wear. Have you seen her anywhere?"

"No, I haven't!" Anna Khordoa snapped.

"I'm in here, Kierky!" a voice called from down the hallway, and the king's daughter-in-law appeared from another door. "I wanted you to wear the blue one. It matches your eyes, my squish muffin."

"I think I'm going to gag," I said.

Anna Khordoa threw her hands up in the air.

"Who's your friend?" Crown Prince Kierkin asked sharply, looking past her at me. "Why does she look so familiar?"

"That's a woman wearing a draft officer's cape!" Princess Orrial gasped. "That's an outrage! Women can't be drafted! It's very offe—"

"Get going!" Anna Khordoa shouted, shoving me towards the door to the throne room.

I fell against the door and yanked the handle. It got stuck once, then twice, then a third time, then a fourth time. The thirteenth time, it finally opened.

I burst into the throne room at the exact moment that there was a lull between two children crying, four young women yelling, and five soldiers bellowing. Six older soldiers were trying to placate the sobbing kids, ten other young women were standing around watching, and the oldest of the three small girls was inching towards the outer doorway. Everyone turned to look at me.

"Here by order of the king," I said immediately. "The children need to go back to their families right now. I'll take them."

I didn't wait for anyone to see through my obvious lie. I just ran forward, grabbed a hand of each of the little girls, jerked them both up to their feet, and raced towards the entrance, dragging them after me. The ten-year-old girl was already well ahead.

"Stop!" Crown Prince Kierkin shouted from behind me. "She's a liar! It's that troublemaking potential child of prophecy!"

There were swords being drawn, young women shouting behind us, and then we reached a line of guards with spears held out in front of us, barring our escape.

"Really," the voice of Crown Prince Kierkin panted from behind us, sounding angry, "what did you think you were doing?"

I noticed the ten-year-old had already fled out into the crowd beyond the four guards holding spears in front of us. I let go of the other two girls' hands, but they only cowered beside me, not taking their chance to escape.

"There they are!" I shouted, pointing off to the left. "The Geminans!"

All four of the guards' heads whipped that way, and I ducked under the line of spears and burst out the other side.

"Stop her!" the crown prince bellowed.

But the crowd had heard me, and everyone was panicking, racing in one direction or another. I yanked off my unwanted cape and flung it out behind me, where I hoped it would get trampled.

I hid behind one of my favorite garbage receptacles to root through, a huge one near the castle where the king and his kin regularly disposed of barely-broken furniture, and waited for the guards and soldiers to thunder by. Then I slipped out and headed through the back alleys to reach the street where my family lived.

"Did they ask me who my family was?" I muttered as I walked. "No, they didn't. Good. They'd have to check the census to find which families have a Henina, and there must be dozens who have my name."

Too late, I realized I might have just given the Fates a helpful hint. If the guards searched through the census records at random, rather than methodically, I might be the first Henina they'd find.

"Oh, well," I said. "I still need breakfast. I'm hungry."

CHAPTER 13

THIRTEEN GRIDDLE CAKES AND A GREEDY SISTER

Dorry, my younger brother, was the one to open the door.

"Ma!" he shouted. "Henina's home! And she didn't even bring any useful garbage with her!"

Ma appeared from the kitchen with her hands on her hips. "Henina!" she scolded. "Where have you been? It's been nearly two days! What were you doing all night last night?"

I stared at her incredulously. "I was picked as a potential child of prophecy? I've been trapped in the castle? Did you not notice?"

"What prophecy?" Orran asked, squeezing between Ma and Dorry. "You mean the one from Prophecy Day?"

"Yes, the one from Prophecy Day!" I exclaimed. "The one about stopping the war! Can I come in now?"

They got out of the way, and I crowded into the house, fuming. They hadn't even noticed that I'd been abducted by the king's guards? What kind of family were they?

"It's been very quiet while you were gone," Veiet said. "Maybe you should get married so you can live somewhere else."

"But who'd want to marry her?" Orran cackled.

Dorry cracked up.

"So glad you missed me," I said acidly. "Glad to know that while I was in terrible danger at every minute, you were all just enjoying the peace and quiet for once."

"Aw, c'mon, we didn't know you were in danger," Dorry protested.

"What kind of danger?" Ma asked sharply. She had the same haunted look in her eyes that she did whenever we mentioned Darson, our oldest brother, who'd been killed in the war.

"Never mind," I said quickly. "It's not important. I need griddle cakes for breakfast."

"Yes!" Dorry shouted, jumping up and down. "Griddle cakes! Those are impossibly good!"

Ma put her hands on her hips. "I only make those for special occasions, we barely have any beet sugar left, and they're not a breakfast food!"

"Which only makes them more impossible, which is why I need them," I said. "Ma, please? It's important for my safety today."

"Well . . ." Ma wavered.

"I don't think you know what 'impossible' means," Veiet said.

"It means 'shut up unless you want me to hit you,'" I shot back.

"Maaaa!" Veiet complained.

"I'll make the cakes," Ma said, cutting through her. "But after that, will you explain what this is about?"

Ma hurried to the kitchen, which was really just a back corner of our open front room, and Pa appeared from the back room, which was where we kept our storefront. We fed the street urchins there, too, because Ma hated having the sticky-fingered scamps anywhere near our private possessions. She'd lost her best pan to one of them.

"I'm three days behind without your help," he said. "I don't suppose you've got time to sharpen a pair of formerly-broken shears?"

"Sorry, Pa, I don't know how long I'll be here before I have to take off again," I said. Then I thought better of it. "Well, if I don't know, I may as well get started. Bring 'em to me."

He beamed and ducked into the back room that was both workshop and storefront.

"What do you mean, before you have to take off again?" Dorry demanded. "Where are you going? You live here."

"I dunno if I still do," I said. "I might have to take off until somebody else stops the war. Which might happen today, given where everyone's going."

"Henina, what is going *on*?" Ma burst out, stirring the bowl full of lumpy batter tucked between her elbow and chest vigorously.

"Lemme start the fire for you," I said, jumping up and tossing a candle stub into the fireplace next to a lump of half-finished wood. I grabbed the firesteel and the rather battered rock we kept beside it, and began smashing the rock against the steel. Sparks caught the wood, and a tiny fire licked up.

"Here are the shears," Pa said, holding a pair of rusty shears and a whetstone out to me as I stood. "There's a seamstress who wants to buy these from me later today."

"Even with the rust?" I asked skeptically. "These need to be scrubbed clean."

"Scrub brush got stolen," Pa said. "Don't worry, she's willing to pay half price even if she has to scrub it herself."

Annoyed, I started sharpening the first blade on the whetstone. "You'd think the scamps could keep their sticky fingers to themselves occasionally."

"You're the one who hires them!" Ma snapped.

Veiet flung her hands over her ears as if to block out the impending, and very likely, argument.

"Ma, I'm not a peacemaker, right?" I asked, since that reminded me of another thing.

She snorted. "What? Did somebody say you were?"

"Nah," I said, "just checking. 'Cause I think I'd be a very bad choice to stop a war, and that's what the child of prophecy's supposed to do."

Orran snickered behind his hand.

"Yeah, I know!" I shouted at him.

"So that's why you wanna take off?" Pa asked. "So you don't have to stop the war?"

"Yeah," I said. "'Cause the only way I can think of that I might stop it would be to cause a worse disaster. I don't wanna do that. Better to leave it to the other twenty-three girls. They'd do it better than me."

"I think," Pa said, "that you could learn to do anything you set your mind to. Even keeping your mouth shut."

"I don't wanna learn to keep my mouth shut," I said. "I think better when I'm talking aloud. I don't wanna be afraid, either, and I figure that's the only thing that would keep me silent."

Pa looked amused, but nodded. "Sounds like you."

I heard a sizzle, and glanced over to see Ma pouring batter onto the griddle, which she'd set over the fire. Delicious aroma drifted up from that direction. There wasn't a lot of batter, so she poured out thirteen small griddle cakes that all fit at once. They bubbled on top, so she flipped them over.

"I want four," Dorry shouted. "No, I want six!"

"You can't have half of them!" Orran shot back.

Veiet threw her hands over her ears.

"You can't have six because I have to have ten," I said.

Mouths opened in indignation all around me.

"You can't have ten!" Orran cried.

"You are so greedy!" Dorry shouted.

"I have to have ten impossible things for breakfast!" I shouted back. "Oh, besides which, that reminds me. This doesn't count as breakfast because I didn't actually swallow it." I reached into the hidden pocket underneath my armpit and pulled out the ruby. "I figure this should be worth a few tins. Maybe even a silver. You could buy more beet sugar with that, right?"

Ma gasped. "Is that . . .?"

"A ruby," I said, and I smelled the faint scent of char. "Ma, the griddle cakes!"

She spun around and quickly flipped each of them onto a plate. She brought the plate over, still steaming. The impossibly good smell wafted up, and my mouth watered.

"Where did you get that from?" Ma demanded. "Did you steal it?"

"The self-important charlatan knows I have it, and she let me keep it," I said with great dignity. "Actually, she thinks I ate it, but it makes no difference to her. Here, this should help out, shouldn't it?" I shoved the ruby into Ma's hand.

Ma stared at the ruby uncertainly. "I'm not sure . . ."

I wolfed down two, then three, griddle cakes. I helped myself to my fourth, fifth, and sixth.

"It's so unfair," Dorry muttered.

I savored my seventh, sweet on the inside and crackly on the outside, and was starting to feel full by the eighth.

"If you had to eat ten impossible things, couldn't it have been ten *pieces* of just one griddle cake?" Orran demanded.

"I didn't think of that, but yes, it probably could have," I agreed, stuffing the ninth one into my mouth. I chewed, swallowed, and then took my tenth. "Too late now, though."

"Greedy sister," Dorry muttered.

I finished my tenth griddle cake and pushed the plate over to them. "There you go. There's one left for each of you."

They all glared at me.

"Hey, it's not any worse than when Darson, Elayn, Adarr, and Carran all lived at home," I defended.

Ma's eyes watered a little, like they always did when someone mentioned Darson.

"Oh, sorry, Ma," I said regretfully. "I shouldn't have mentioned him, especially not during a draft day."

"What?" Pa asked alarmed. "What do you mean? It's not a draft day!"

"Uh oh," I said. A knot appeared in my stomach. "You mean there hasn't been an official announcement yet? King Derroll's running a special draft today so that he has some excuse to drag all the potential children of prophecy to the front lines. Uh, maybe you should hide Orran and Dorry, just in case . . ."

A thunderous knock came at the front door.

"Out the back door," Dad said rapidly, grabbing my brothers and shoving them towards the workshop. "Now!"

The front door burst open, and two men with swords wearing the hated, hated capes were standing there.

"Orran son-of-Dar and Dorry son-of-Dar, we have the honor to inform you . . ." one of them began.

Ma screamed, and Veiet launched herself at one of the men, sinking her teeth into his arm.

"Ow!" the man shouted.

"They're escaping through the back!" the other man called, charging into the house. He came back holding each of my brothers by a pinched ear.

Ma burst into tears.

CHAPTER 14

FOURTEEN WAYS TO SAVE MY BROTHERS

oth of my brothers. Both of my brothers who were eligible for the draft had been called up. This was not a coincidence. Or rather, it was, and I passionately hated the Fates for it.

Ma wept as they were marched away. I merely seethed inside.

"The Fates are trying to motivate me," I told Pa, clenching my fists. "It's working."

"Henina," he said, and swallowed, then swallowed again, "don't do anything dangerous. For your ma's sake, at least. Please."

"I'm not gonna let that idiotic war kill two more brothers!" I snapped. "Ma, stop crying! If I have to be the child of prophecy to save them both, I'll do it, but I'm gonna make sure they get back here alive. You hear me?"

Ma nodded, but the tears still poured down her face.

Veiet let out a choking sob, and she started crying, too. Pa's eyes watered, and he looked like he was about to collapse in on himself.

"Pa," I said, turning to him, "you said I could do anything I set my mind to. Have some faith."

"Wh-what are you going to do?" Veiet stammered.

"I'm gonna —" I stopped. "You know what? I don't even have to make plans. If I'm doing what the Fates want, they'll make it very easy for me. I'll see you when I get back."

I opened the front door.

"Wait —" Ma cried.

I stepped outside and slammed the door after me.

"Hey!" I called, storming down the empty streets. When the draft officers were out, everyone cowered in their homes, and today would be worse than ever because it had been unexpected. "Is there anyone coincidentally out looking for me? It's me, Henina! The troublesome potential child of prophecy who ran away!"

I heard thudding footsteps and the clatter of steel in a scabbard, and a very familiar-looking guard appeared around a corner. He ran over, seized my arm triumphantly, and began to march me back to the castle.

"Yes, yes, you're so amazing," I said. "Your shoe is clinking. How many silvers of draft dodge money did you collect today?"

His face turned red and he said nothing.

"Did the Fates decide to motivate me, or was it the king?" I added, thinking about it. "If it was His Majesty, I have a few extra special words for him."

The guard said nothing, continuing to march with me.

"That's all right, I'll just assume it was both of them," I said. "His Majesty's to blame for the draft existing in the first place."

When we got to the castle, I was locked into a room with all of the other potentials. Even the ten-year-old who had escaped seemed to have been caught. Most of the girls looked stunned. Some of them were weeping.

"Why did you come back?" Anna Khordoa greeted me. "You were supposed to get lost."

"Tried that, went home, found out my brothers got drafted," I said. "Came back."

"*All* of our brothers did!" a girl wailed. "Or our fathers, or uncles — whoever was eligible!"

One of the girls let out a loud, high-pitched sob that resembled the shriek of a hoarse bird of prey. Another one, not to be outdone, let out a howl like a whining thunderstorm.

"Right," I said, irritated. "Stop all this. You can't possibly be more upset than I am — both of my unmarried brothers got drafted, and I know how bad that is because another of my brothers died in the war years ago."

"My sweetheart got drafted, and we were supposed to be married next week!" a third girl howled.

". . . Right," I said. "Okay, I take it back. You can be more upset than I am."

"And my little brother just turned twelve last month!" another girl wailed.

"And my —"

"And my —"

"And my —"

Sob stories clamored over each other, demanding to be heard.

I held up my hands. "I take back my take-back! Nobody has the right to be sad! We should all be *angry*."

Everyone stared at me.

"But —" one girl started.

"No!" I snapped. "We are all potential children of prophecy. And do you know what we were prophesied to do? *Stop the war.* And you know when we are going to do that? Today. Before anybody's brother or father or uncle or sweetheart gets killed. Got it?!"

Hiccups rang all over the room. Forty-six eyes were fastened on me.

"But we don't know who —" one of the girls began.

"Then we'll *all* do it," I said. "Let somebody else worry about who the child of prophecy is. For now, all that matters is saving our families."

Girls sat up straight. Hope dawned in many of their eyes.

Anna Khordoa looked away.

"Oh, don't think you're immune to this just because you're rich!" I snapped. "Maybe your family can afford to pay for draft dodge money, but do you really think that will deter the Fates? One way or another, they're going to get someone you care about on that battlefield. They're rotten, stinking cheaters, and whatever power you think you have, they're better."

Thunder rumbled outside. Gasps rang across the room.

Anna Khordoa sighed heavily. She folded her arms. "You were supposed to not offend anyone else important today."

"That doesn't really matter anymore," I said. "Besides, the prediction didn't guarantee I would be the child of prophecy if I didn't do those things, only that I wouldn't if I did. The only thing that really matters is who stops the war, and we're all going to do it. Together."

One girl asked timidly, "How?"

I shrugged. "I dunno. I could think of fourteen ways to save my brothers, and not one of them would make a single difference. You know why? Because the Fates care about what happens, which means any plan could succeed or fail depending on their whims."

The fortune teller who was not named Helga said quietly from the back, "Nevertheless, we should still have a plan. When the story is told later, the Fates won't want it to sound like we did nothing but sit back and wait for their aid. That would make for a boring play."

One of the girls gasped. "Do you think there's going to be a play about us?"

"Indubitably," Anna Khordoa smiled, leaning forward. "I'll pay to have it funded myself."

"With yourself as the main character, no doubt," I said.

"Well, who else would it be?" she demanded. "I am —"

"— very sure of yourself, yep, we know that," I said. "So? Who's with me?"

Heads nodded around the room. One young woman stood up. Another two followed her. Soon even the small girls were standing. Only Anna Khordoa remained seated.

"We need all of us to do this to work," I told her with some annoyance.

"You try to stop the war in your little way; I'll try to stop the war in mine," she said. "The Fates will have to choose between us, and I want it to be unambiguous that I am the child of prophecy when mine is the one they pick."

"Okay," I snorted. "As long as we're working simultaneously, the Fates will have to pick something, so you probably won't be too much in the way."

"In that case, we want to do it on our own, too," a young woman declared, gesturing to three others around her. "My roommates and I have a plan that we think will work."

"No," I said, "you're missing the point. It'll be best if we all work together, because that will guarantee that any plan will succeed —"

"I don't want to keep on being a *potential* child of prophecy!" another girl complained. "I want it to be certain! I want all the rest of you to be eliminated so that everyone knows it's me!"

"Yeah!"

"Uh huh!"

"Me, too!"

"Also, if we follow your plan, that'll just mean you were the one really responsible for ending the war, which would mean we're all eliminated anyway!" another girl exclaimed.

I stared around the room in incredulity. "A minute ago you were all crying, and now you're trying to stab each other in the back? What's *wrong* with you people?"

Hostile glares met my innocent inquiry.

"I think you just lost control of the room," Anna Khordoa said with amusement. "That's not the sort of thing that someone who's destined to rule would be doing."

CHAPTER 15

FIFTEEN DIFFERENT PLANS RUNNING AMUCK

Quickly, the room dissolved into a seething mass of alliances, betrayals, and counterplots, while I stared in mystification at the intrigue before me.

"Your suggestion did work in one sense," the fortune teller said, standing beside my side. "Everyone is now too busy plotting to continue worrying, and nobody seems to be planning to try to run away. Even the children seem eager to contribute."

"Terrific," I said. "That's exactly what I was hoping to achieve."

"Weren't you, though?" the fortune teller asked. "So they haven't pulled together in one large group effort. We're all still going to be trying to stop the war at the same time. Regardless of what plan the Fates choose, the results will be the same."

I eyed a group of three young women who were huddled together, whispering among themselves and occasionally making stabbing motions to punctuate their words.

"There's at least one plan that doesn't seem to be nonviolent," I said. "And the Fates only need one of us to be alive at the end. What if the war ends because everyone's disgusted that a bunch of children and young women were brutally slaughtered after they charged the enemy's front lines in desperation to save their brothers and sweethearts? What if that's the king's plan for us today?"

"You were the one who said the plan didn't matter, as long as the Fates stop the war today," the fortune teller reminded me.

"I think it's pretty obvious I was wrong," I said.

Keys rattled in a lock, and the door to our locked room opened. Every potential fell silent as a line of guards stood there, watching us.

"We're gonna stop the war now!" the four-year-old declared.

Without being asked, the room's occupants began to line up to be filed out. Anna Khordoa was in front, looking smug.

"Well, of course she's smug, because she doesn't have to worry that the king will use her as a martyr," I pondered out loud. "Unless, of course, King Derroll thinks she's too ambitious and would like to see her removed from a position where she could threaten his sons' power. Come to think of it, that might make her a perfect martyr."

Anna Khordoa shot me a poisonous look as we were marched out of the room. Some of the other girls looked very nervous.

"Nervousness is only natural," I commented as we were herded down the hallway. "Terror would be even more natural."

The guards marched us into the throne room, where the king was sitting ominously on his gleaming goldwood throne.

"That chair's not very structurally sound," I said. "I don't know if you've noticed, but the legs are starting to puddle a bit at the bottom. And speaking of bottoms, how big is yours? It has to be large because that chair was very uncomfortable when I sat on it."

"Silence!" the king roared, standing.

"You've known me for two days now. You must know that's impossible," I said. "Oh, huh, maybe I could have tried to swallow ten comments instead of eating something literal for breakfast. Yeah, that might have been what the self-important charlatan meant. Well, her fault for being so vague, and I'm glad I ate the griddle cakes and ruby."

"Silence!" the king roared again.

Two guards beside me drew their swords.

"Silence, or you will be silenced," the king added dangerously.

"Then you won't know which one of us is the spy for Gemina," I said. "It's not me, by the way."

The king was silent for a moment. The guards continued to hold their swords out.

"Who?" King Derroll growled finally.

"I won't say," I said. "It's my insurance that none of us get killed."

"I don't believe you could hold it back," the king snarled.

"Do you want to rest all your plans on the assumption that I wouldn't lie if you forced it out of me?" I asked. "It's not the one you're thinking of, by the way."

"And which one is that?" he asked sarcastically.

"Anna Khordoa," I said. "Your eyes flicked over at her when I said that. It's not the fortune teller who's not named Helga, either. Or the one with the black curls. Or that one. Or that one. Or that one. Oh, you're looking around the room to get me to eliminate all the suspects. Fine, I'll stop paying attention to where you're looking."

"Who is it?!" the king roared.

"One of the others," I said. "Stop looking around. It's very distracting. I want us all to come back from the war alive, and everyone else you're taking out there today."

"You're not getting out of going there," the king growled.

"No, of course not," I said. "Why would I want that? We're all going to go. It's just that we're going to follow our own plans, not your plan to use us as martyrs and bait. Oh, so that *was* your plan?" I asked as his face turned bright red. "Yes, I figured it was. I'm not sure how you thought that would get around the 'ruling with wisdom and grace' thing, but — oh, wait, you only needed to keep Asaya alive and marry her off to one of your sons. Right."

"That was not my plan!" he barked.

"Well, if not, it should have been," I said. "You didn't think of such an obvious strategy that would have benefited you? What's wrong with you? If you're going to be selfish and greedy, you ought to at least be good at it."

The king's fingers tapped the air twitchily. He noticed me watching his hand and stopped, glaring at me.

"Now you're mad at me, but you really shouldn't be mad when I'm just telling you what everybody else thinks," I said. "Nobody wants the war and everyone hates the draft officers, and by the way, most of the deserters wind up working for crime lords, and at least one of those is planning a revolution. I know because two separate people have tried to recruit Pa, which he always refused, but he said I should keep it a secret anyway." I paused. "Oops."

The king was deadly silent.

"If you really want to stay king, you should make sure to take all the credit for ending the war and then do something really generous for the common people that the Fates haven't forced you to," I said. "Throwing six silvers out into the crowd was good, but only six people benefited from that. Maybe you could throw seventy-two tins out into the crowd instead, or five hundred and seventy-six coppers, or nine thousand, two hundred and sixteen irons."

The king said nothing.

"You should ask the self-important charlatan for advice," I said. "That's what I call your fortune teller because she's self-important and a charlatan, but she might still have some good advice. This morning she read the stones for me and told me a few things I knew already and a few more that weren't feasible, and she was vague enough to give herself plenty of room for interpretation just in case I fulfilled all the things she said and she still turned out to be wrong, but that's pretty much the best you can expect." I paused. "I'm pretty sure your soothsayer's the same way. Maybe you need some new advisors."

"You want to follow your own plans at the battlefront?" the king said. "Fine. You can follow your own plans. As long as Gemina doesn't win, you can do whatever you please without consequences. If they do win, you will all be executed, and your entire families, as well. Are we clear?"

Gasps and whispers and moans rose up all around me.

"Sure, as long as we'll *all* be executed," I said with a grin. "As long as that's guaranteed, it'll cut off the path that Gemina can win. Smart thinking. Will you put that all in writing, so we can't escape it?"

"It will be my pleasure," the king said with a mocking smile.

"Mine, too," I said, "because the 'no consequences' part that you said and that everyone here heard and that you'd better commit to writing too really opens up some interesting possibilities."

The smile dropped from the king's face.

"Well, we'd better go now," I said. "I've heard the battlefront's about a day's walk from here, which is why deserters usually congregate in the city, so it should be only a few hours by carriage. The sooner we get there, the sooner we can put our plans in motion without consequences, which is a nice freedom. You're all welcome."

Hostile looks surrounded me.

"By the way, there will be fifteen different plans running amuck," I said, "so you might want to warn your generals or whoever's there to stay out of our way unless they want to be pulled into it. Oh, and give us all authority in writing to do whatever we please, would you? We're going to need that to get anyone to listen to us. I'll check to make sure you wrote exactly what you said, and we'll bring it with us."

The king moved slowly, but he stepped down from the throne and gestured for a servant to get paper.

"Hey, Anna Khordoa," I said, turning to grin at her. "It looks like you never gained control of this room in the first place. That's not the sort of thing that someone who's destined to rule would be doing."

SIXTEEN POSSIBLE TRAITORS, AND ONE MAYBE

Not long after that, we were taken to a line of carriages. Anna Khordoa, Asaya, and I were all stuffed into the first, presumably because we were considered most important.

"I never attempted to take control of that room," Anna Khordoa informed me as soon as we were alone in the carriage with a guard standing outside the door to make sure we didn't try to escape, "because to do so would be stupid. You, for instance, managed to get my uncle to agree to kill us all if we fail."

"What, don't you have faith we'll succeed?" I asked.

She snorted.

"You like to keep your options open," I noted. "Well, I'd rather failure not be an option. You may not have any family members going off to war today, but I do."

"Wh-who's the traitor?" Asaya whispered, leaning forward. "Who's the spy for Gemina?"

"I just made that up," I said. "Possibly none of us."

"You made that *up?*" Anna Khordoa asked in a strangled voice.

I shrugged. "It kept the king from killing me, didn't it?"

"What are you going to say if he asks who the traitor was after it's over?" she hissed.

"How should I know?" I asked. "I'll probably say the first thing that pops into my head. Mind you, it does seem plausible, since the Fates like to keep their options open, too."

"So that's sixteen people who are now in danger because of your mouth," Anna Khordoa hissed. "Terrific!"

"Seventeen," I said. "Your count is off. I only eliminated seven, including me. And why do you care? You were one of them."

"My count is not off," Anna Khordoa said stiffly, "because Asaya is above suspicion."

"You realize that if this were a play, that would guarantee she was a traitor," I said. I eyed the other rich girl suspiciously. "Are you?"

The timid girl's eyes filled with tears.

"That's not an argument to the contrary," I said.

Asaya sniffled and buried her face in her hands.

"Now that you've offended yet another important person," Anna Khordoa said impatiently, "I'll explain to you that she's above suspicion because her father's one of the generals, and she's always been watched extremely carefully to guard against that sort of thing."

"Oh," I said. "Okay, so that leaves sixteen possible traitors, and one maybe."

Asaya sobbed again.

"Either those tears are fake and manipulative, or they're genuine and ridiculous," I told Anna Khordoa. "How can you stand it?"

"It's considered the ideal for rich girls to be that 'sensitive,'" Anna Khordoa told me. "She's not the only one that easily hurt. One of the reasons you should never, ever wind up ruling."

"Appalling," I commented. "Gives me another reason to dislike you rich people, gotta say."

"Why are you talking about me as if I'm not here?" Asaya wailed.

"Because your crying for no reason is extremely irritating, and Anna Khordoa just smirked slightly, so she thinks so, too," I said.

Asaya hiccuped and sat back, sniffling.

There was a whipping sound in front of us, and our carriage lurched forward.

"Guess the guard's sitting up front with the driver," I said. "Think they thought to leave us any food here?"

Asaya hesitated, and then removed some flat-looking bread pockets from her sleeves. "I — I saved these from breakfast — because I thought the food at the battlefront might be awful — if you two want them?"

"Now *that's* smart thinking," I approved. "You should keep them. You might need them."

She hesitated, and then shook her head. "I had a plan, but mine was awful. You're right. I'm too easily hurt. I should never have wanted to rule or be the child of prophecy. I'll never be anything useful."

"I never said any of that, and if you have weaknesses, so what?" I retorted. "So do I. So does Anna Khordoa. And her jerkiness is stronger than either of our weaknesses put together."

"It is not!" Anna Khordoa snapped.

Asaya smiled tremulously. "So you really think that — I could do it?"

"I think that you should try, and I'll root for you over Anna Khordoa," I said. I paused. "Of course, I'd root for anyone over Anna Khordoa. She likely feels the same way about me."

"No, I'll only root for myself," she snorted.

"Like I said, jerkiness," I said. "It's amazing how much I don't like you."

"Can I — can I tell you my plan, Henina?" Asaya asked tentatively. "Since you might help me know if anything's wrong?"

"If you want Anna Khordoa to know about it too, and possibly sabotage you," I said.

"She won't do that," Asaya said. "I know what her plan is, and if she sabotages my plan, it'll sabotage hers, too." She took a deep breath. "I think we should surrender."

"You realize that'll amount to losing the war," I said.

"I'm not done yet." She swallowed. "I think we should surrender, and then, when they come in to discuss terms, we kill all their leaders."

I stared at her, aghast. "That's . . . really brutal."

"I know," she said tentatively, "but they won't expect it from us because we're fragile, innocent girls thrown into a war zone against our will who are destined to stop the war, and they'll think we've ended it once we surrender."

"I suppose that could work," I said slowly, "but it could also make things much worse."

Anna Khordoa gave me a brittle smile. "That kind of hesitance to do what's necessary is why the war has been prolonged fifty years. The obvious thing is to break the rules of engagement."

"And to fight dirty," Asaya said, nodding. "Both sides agreed thirty-nine years ago that they will only send in reinforcements twice a year and allow anyone who's injured to go home. King Derroll's already breaking the first one. We should definitely break the second and attack Gemina's medical camp if they don't surrender after we kill all their leaders. That'll break the spirits of anyone who's left."

"Are you *kidding?*" I shouted.

"We don't have to worry about consequences," Anna Khordoa said coolly. "You saw to that. We can use whatever tactics we want, and we'll just be hailed as heroines for ending the war."

"And it's better that their soldiers die than more of ours do," Asaya said, nodding. "We might normally need to worry that they'd hustle reinforcements over and the war would just escalate, thereby resulting in the mutual extermination of both of our populations, but the thing is, the Fates said that the war would end."

My mouth was dry. "Mutual extermination would qualify."

"It's worth the risk," Anna Khordoa said. "The prophecy makes that unlikely. It would be difficult for any of us to rule if both Gemina and Horhold were exterminated."

"And we're very tiny kingdoms," Asaya agreed. "With shrinking populations. Even if both sides exterminate the other, there are only a few hundred thousand civilians left on either side. More than that many soldiers have died in the past fifty years already. From a mathematical standpoint, it's definitely necessary."

I gaped at her. "What happened to the timid wallflower who was easily offended? I want *her* back, and I never thought I'd say that!"

Asaya's eyes filled with tears. "Do you really think it won't work?"

"Ignore her," Anna Khordoa said. "It's a great plan, and I don't usually compliment people. I never thought you had it in you, but you might be a great choice to marry one of my cousins. As long as it's just Horhold you want, I won't stand in your way."

Asaya's face lit up.

I put my hands to my head. "I can't believe I wanted to make you the child of prophecy. You're just as bad as Anna Khordoa!"

Asaya's lower lip trembled.

"That's a compliment," Anna Khordoa told her.

"No, it isn't," I shot back.

Asaya nodded and wiped her eyes and somehow managed to keep them dry.

"I'm going to try to stop both of you," I said. "It's amazing, but I think I hate you both equally. Well, no. Anna Khordoa still wins out. But just barely."

"You won't stand a chance," Anna Khordoa said confidently.

"Watch me offend every important person I meet at the battlefield," I shot back. "I'm sure there'll be lots of them."

SEVENTEEN IMPORTANT PEOPLE TO OFFEND ON PURPOSE

Jumping down from the carriage as soon as we reached a place that looked like an old town that had been converted to a permanent battle camp, Anna Khordoa stepped out of the carriage, held high the writ I had brought from the king, and announced, "Your salvation is here! I, Anna Khordoa, the child of the prophecy, shall be ending the war today!"

Asaya nervously poked her head out and said, "U-um, me too . . ."

"So am I, and so are twenty-one other girls and young woman traveling behind us," I said, glancing back. "Oh, look, the second one's arriving. They'll probably say the same thing as soon as their door's unlocked and they come out."

A pack of soldiers gathered around us, staring at us in mystification.

"Hi, I'm Henina, potential child of prophecy," I said to the nearest. "Are you important? If so, what can I do to offend you today?"

He stared at my hand. "I'm not easily offended . . ."

"Well, then I hope you're not important," I said.

"Not really?" he said.

"Where can I find someone important?" I demanded. "I need to offend them. It's important for my stopping-the-war effort."

He slowly reached over and pointed at a badly-repaired house behind me.

"Thanks!" I said cheerfully, and marched off that direction. Anna Khordoa was still grandly introducing herself.

The door opened, and a man with a red cap opened the door before I could reach it. "What's going on?" he barked.

"Hi, I'm Henina, and I'm here to offend you," I said, holding out my hand. "How can I do that today?"

"*Why are all these women here?!*" he shouted.

"Order of the king!" Anna Khordoa called back, waving the paper above her head. "I have been prophesied to stop the war, and I will be doing that today!"

"What makes you think you can do something that we cannot?" the man demanded furiously. "A few whores in the camp won't make a difference!"

Anna Khordoa's face turned bright red, and she gaped in outrage.

"Because that was immensely satisfying, I'll find somebody else to offend," I said. "Is there anyone more important than you?"

The red-capped man gave me a furious look.

"Oh, guess I offended you after all," I noted.

It took nearly fifteen minutes for all of the carriages to arrive and explanations to be made, and by that point, we were surrounded by hundreds of hopeful soldiers and seventeen red-capped officers who looked either hopeful or exhausted or offended that we were here.

I managed to offend all of them within a few minutes, so I was quickly shunted to stand outside the crowd, where my comments would no longer interrupt everything.

"There sure are a lot of trees out here," I noted to the soldiers around me, all of whom wore shabby clothing, some of whom looked as young as twelve. "They're all pretty short, though. Were they planted specifically to hide the camp from enemy eyes, or did they just grow and nobody cared enough to pull them out of what presumably used to be farmland?"

Nobody answered me. They were all craning their necks to see something. The shorter ones were now standing on tiptoes.

". . . the king's order," Anna Khordoa was saying. "This is his seal. We have the rights to do whatever is necessary, including breaking the rules you have been blindly following for fifty years."

I didn't want to hear her explaining the awful ideas she'd agreed with Asaya about on the way here, so I edged away from the crowd.

There were lines of laundry strung up, a halfhearted garden that looked picked bare, and an appallingly odoriferous outhouse that I choked and stepped away from, slamming the door.

"No ideas there," I said. I ambled past a fire pit that was currently cold, with a flint and firesteel left there for convenience, and wandered back to the crowd.

"I've heard from a former soldier that your time at the front is nine-tenths mind-numbing boredom and one-tenth sheer terror," I commented to one of the men at the edge. "Is that true?"

"Shh!" one of the men hissed at me, barely glancing back. "Yes. Let me hear."

Asaya was now trying to get a word in edgewise, but Anna Khordoa kept cutting her off. One of the other girls spoke up and started to explain her plan, which seemed to involve scarecrows to keep the enemies busy while the the real soldiers snuck into their camp across the barren clearing and took their leaders hostage.

Laughter and jeering soon resulted, bursting across the crowd.

Another voice rose up, and a young woman was explaining that if they just calmly told everyone the war was over, everyone would go home —

More laughter and jeering.

Asaya tried to speak up, but Anna Khordoa's voice rose high above hers. "Henina! Is your plan less ridiculous, or is it more so?"

"I don't know yet!" I called back, causing half the crowd to glance back at me. "I'll tell you when I come up with one!"

More laughter and jeering.

Another young woman's voice rose up, and she spoke about using clotheslines to trip up the whole enemy's army at once —

An explosion of laughter that was twice as loud as before.

An idea struck my mind. I ran over to the cold fire pit and scooped up the flint and firesteel. I wasn't sure which way the mine was, but it was probably somewhere in the mountain off to the left, which looked only about a five minute walk away.

"There have to be soldiers guarding it," I said, "probably from both sides, otherwise the mine would have been picked clean by one of the sides already. Oh, look, laundry."

I set down the firesteel and flint and felt along the clothesline, finding shirts and pants that were dry and leaving the damp ones behind.

Once I had enough, I awkwardly bent down to pick up the firesteel and flint, and laundry tumbled out of my arms onto the dirt.

"What are you doing?" one of the men asked, noticing me. Several others turned around to watch, too.

"Just doing your laundry that fell in the dirt," I said. "It relaxes me. I need that to come up with a plan. Which way is the river?"

The soldiers laughed, very relaxed and amused, as they pointed off towards the left.

"Perfect," I said. "I'll go take care of things there."

I headed off in that direction purposefully. Several of the men were watching me go, but then a girl's voice said huffily from the center of the crowd that no one better laugh at her plan because it was brilliant, and if they just listened to her, then they would know —

You could practically feel the anticipation building.

I waited until the men were all craning their necks to watch her, and then ran back to scoop up the firesteel and flint I'd dropped. I stuffed them into the middle of the bundle of clothes, where they wouldn't be as noticeable and suspicious, and then ambled off with pure innocence that would have been highly suspicious to anyone that knew me.

I passed several isolated soldiers fishing in the river, some of whom gave me annoyingly lecherous looks. I waved cheerfully to the polite ones and informed the rude ones that there were a bunch of women in the camp right now, letting them draw their own conclusions. One of them dropped his fishing pole and ran back to the abandoned village posthaste.

I stopped to pick up the bucket of fish he'd left on the bank. I had to slide my arm through the handle so that I could still carry the laundry with the firesteel and flint hidden inside, but it wasn't too unwieldy once I got used to it.

"Where are you taking the fish?" the next soldier I passed asked me.

"Lunch for the soldiers guarding the mine," I said. "Which way is it?"

He pointed.

"Thank you!" I beamed.

I was getting the feeling that these men were not always as lonely as the former soldiers in the city complained they had been.

"Darson had better have behaved during the years he was here," I muttered.

I soon reached a cliff face that had a hole dug into it, which had two distinct, smaller camps parked outside it. One was on our side of the mountain; the other was on the other side. Four bored soldiers were lounging on each side. If it hadn't been for the recent bloodstains I passed on the ground as I neared them, the scene would have looked downright pastoral.

I shuddered.

"Hello!" One of the soldiers on our side of the gold mine brightened. "We don't often get women out here!"

"You probably shouldn't get women out near the battlefield at all," I said sourly.

"Are you somebody's wife?" the guy asked, grinning, elbowing his neighbor in the stomach. "Is it your wife, Doby?"

The Geminan soldiers on the other side leaned forward, looking entertained.

"Do you realize how stupid this war is?" I asked in exasperation. "All of you men should be at home, raising your children or at least doing something useful like growing food. Exactly what do you do out here, besides die?"

"We hope to get injured, so we can go home," one of the Geminan soldiers joked.

All the rest of them laughed.

"Why don't you all injure yourselves, then?" I asked.

"We couldn't do that. It would be dishonorable," one of the Horholdan soldiers said, looking insulted.

"That'd be no better than deserting," a Geminan soldier agreed. "You have to obey the rules of combat."

Stupid, stupid, *stupid*.

"What about stealing gold from the mine?" I asked innocently. "Is that allowed?"

"Of course not!" one of the Horholdan soldiers said. "We would never enter it!"

"Never?" I asked. "Not even to take a single piece?"

"Never," a Geminan soldier said firmly.

"Because it's against the rules?" I asked.

"Because it's against the rules," he confirmed.

"The rules sound really strict," I said, walking just close enough to the entrance to peer down into it with wide, innocent eyes. I set down the bucket of fish and leaned forward.

"They are," a Horholdan soldier said, looking a little on-edge. He got to his feet. "If you would please move away . . ."

"Too late!" I beamed and dashed into the mouth of the mine. As I ran, the laundry shifting and the firesteel whamming uncomfortably against my chest, I couldn't resist adding:

"And now I know you can't follow me!"

EIGHTEEN VERY SENSIBLE CHUNKS OF GOLD

ootsteps pounded behind me, but amazingly, they really didn't follow me in.

"Get out of there right now!" one of the soldiers shouted from the entrance. "If anyone goes in and stays there for longer than one minute, we're under orders to shut up the entrance of the mine and leave them there to starve! We don't want to do that to a nice young lady!"

I tripped over a sprawling skeleton, and landed in the dirt. I stared down at it, appalled.

"Last chance!" another soldier called. "We can't let anyone steal anything from the mine, not even a woman! Please come out now!"

I swallowed, and then swallowed again. The skeleton was hard to take. I rapidly considered doing just that.

"No," I told myself under my breath. "I have to stop the war. This is the only way to do it." Louder, I added, "I broke my ankle! I have to sit here to rest! Please don't block me in here!"

There was some murmuring above me.

A voice said regretfully, "We're very sorry, but orders are orders and rules are rules, you know."

There was a long rumble, and a gigantic stone was rolled over the entrance, blocking out all sunlight.

I started screaming and cursing them. "Why do you even leave the entrance open in the first place?!"

But there was no answer.

After a moment, I managed to get ahold of my panic. I closed my eyes, reminding myself that it didn't really matter that I couldn't see anything, and then I felt along the dirt floor for the firesteel and flint I'd dropped when I'd fallen. I made sparks, too small to see by, but enough to find my way to a torch left on the wall. After a lot of effort, I finally managed to light it.

As the room lit up with a dim glow, I breathed a sigh of relief.

"Well," I said out loud, "the major problem with this plan is, I've blocked off my way of escape. I should probably find another one before I set the whole place on fire."

I wrenched the torch out of the wall bracket, with major difficulty because it was stuck, and then stepped forward into the dirt. The mine hadn't gotten very far down: there was only one room other than the entrance, and tiny gold nuggets gleamed all over the walls. It was obvious to see why two kings had wanted this enough to fight a war over it. It was less obvious why they hadn't managed to make peace and compromise to share the prize already.

I found a pickax still lying in the corner, with the wooden part rotted away, but the steel was still good. It had to have been tempered really well to not have rusted after all these years. I was pretty impressed. I hefted it in my hands, feeling its weight, and thudded it into the wall experimentally. One of the tiny nuggets fell out, caked in a clod of dirt.

"Nice," I commented, picking it up. "It's smaller than a gold coin, and it's likely impure, but it has to be worth at least a silver. If I can find a smelter who will ask no questions, I could probably get half that for this. Getting a few more would be only sensible before I figure out how to leave."

I raised the pickax again and dug out eighteen very sensible chunks of gold. Then I stuffed my pockets full and tucked the smallest in my hidden pocket, just in case the rest got confiscated.

"Now to figure out a way to leave," I said. "If I'd brought the fish with me, I would have food and water, but oh, well. Maybe I can dig my way out."

I picked up the pickax and headed to the top room. The stone was still there, completely sealing off the entrance.

I dug the pickax into the wall next to the stone, working out clumps of clay. I did it again, and again, and again. After a few minutes, I realized I was growing short of breath not only because of the exertion but because I was running out of air.

I cursed and put out the torch. I should have remembered that fire breathed air, just like people. Then I resumed digging in the pitch dark. It was not a happy activity.

I was feeling lightheaded when I finally saw a tiny pinprick of light ahead of me. I dropped the pickax and dove for the pinprick, pushing my mouth against the dirt and inhaling deeply.

In. Out. In. Out. In. Out. Whew, that was so much better.

I could hear muffled voices outside. When I put my ear to the pinprick of light, I could just about make out —

Oh, ugh, Anna Khordoa was here to rescue me?

"King Derroll promised that we would *all* survive," she said fiercely. "*All* of us. And we're allowed to break the rules. You let her out of there right now!"

"King Onnarh never authorized any such thing," a soldier's voice said stiffly. "I'm sorry, but our orders are clear. No one who enters this mine can be allowed to leave it, not until the ownership of the mine has been agreed upon."

"Then let's agree upon it," Anna Khordoa said with exasperation. "Half of the mining rights belong to Horhold; the other half the Gemina. This can be renegotiated at a future date, but nobody else can be killed over it. I have the authority to negotiate for my uncle, so this is legally binding. Do we agree?"

"We don't have the authority to . . ." one of the soldiers protested.

"*Do you want to go home tomorrow or sit here for the rest of your lives?*" she thundered.

There was silence for a moment.

"Technically, we aren't forbidden to negotiate on behalf of our king," one of the soldiers said. "Our orders don't say anything about it."

"And it can be renegotiated at a later date," another one agreed.

More silence for a moment.

"All right," a soldier said, formally. "We accept half-ownership in the gold mine on behalf of Gemina and King Onnarh."

"And I accept half-ownership in the gold mine on behalf of Horhold and King Derroll," Anna Khordoa said. "Now open the entrance."

There were a lot of grunts of exertion, and I hastily brushed dirt away from my lips and ear so that I would look presentable. I arranged a cool, unbothered look on my face.

Light pierced my eyes with painful brightness.

"Ouch!" I yelped, and shielded my eyes. "That completely destroys my attempt to look nonchalant! Ow! Sun right in my eyes! Ow!"

"I knew you were in trouble when I saw you were missing," Anna Khordoa said smugly. "Can't survive on your own, can you?"

"Yes, well," I said grumpily, my eyes adjusted enough to look at her now, which wasn't an improvement, "I thought I'd stop the war while you were standing around talking about it. And I succeeded."

The smile dropped from her face. "What are you talking about?"

"Look around!" I said. "What's left to fight over? I was going to burn down the wooden supports inside the mine to make it collapse so that neither side could have it, but this is much better. We're about two seconds away from a peace treaty, and it's all because of me!"

"*I* negotiated it!" she shouted.

"Um," one of the Horholdan soldiers said, holding up a finger, "if we're at peace, if the ownership of the mine is settled, does that mean we can go in and collect some of the gold ore? For Horhold, of course."

"For Gemina, as well!" another soldier said eagerly.

"As long as you take equal amounts," Anna Khordoa said grandly. "For the next hour only, there will be no restrictions or counting."

Eight men burst past us to run into the mine.

"Of course, we still have to negotiate the truce," I said.

"That'll be harder than you think," Anna Khordoa said, "given that Asaya's plan is already set in motion."

CHAPTER 19

NINETEEN LIARS
FAKING A SURRENDER

You encouraged her!" I shouted at Anna Khordoa as we ran to the battlefield. In the distance, I could see a large white flag being waved. It was probably a bedsheet. "Anything bad that happens now is *your* fault!"

"I kept trying to cut her off!" Anna Khordoa snapped back. "I plan to rule Gemina! Do you think that's going to happen if we escalate the war with her stupid plan?"

"Then why didn't you say that in the carriage?!" I exclaimed.

"Because if her plan had won, I'd want to be in her good graces!" Anna Khordoa snarled, panting beside me. "I was trying to make sure she didn't get a chance to talk, but no, the officers insisted, and then suddenly nobody was laughing, and I waited for you to say something stupid that would defuse the situation, but no, you were gone, and I knew you'd gone to get in trouble somewhere. You're welcome for saving you!"

"Fine, what was *your* plan?" I demanded.

"I was going to get myself taken hostage and forced into an alliance to end the war," Anna Khordoa said promptly. "I'd wind up married to the crown prince of Gemina, the war would be over, and I'd get all the credit for being brave and self-sacrificing. I don't know what Asaya thought I had planned, but I think she's off her rocker."

"Or she's listened to her father about too many things," I said. "You said he's a general. Maybe he's had strong opinions he's vented about at home before."

"Yeah, that could . . . do it," Anna Khordoa agreed, her breath coming in short gasps. "Can we . . . slow down . . . just a little bit?"

"We're almost there," I said, glancing back as she clutched her side. "Don't worry, if I make it there first, I'll take credit for everything."

She glared at me and put on a burst of speed.

We reached the group of nineteen soldiers, seven of them wearing red caps, who were waving the white sheet at the edge of the trees. As we reached them, I caught sight of the thick, muddy clearing of the battlefield for the first time, and my stomach heaved. There were three broken corpses strewn across the empty expanse, two decomposing and one that looked it had only been killed this morning. Flies buzzed around each of them.

"Don't you even bury them?!" I exclaimed.

"Once a week, on burial day," a red-capped man near me said. "That's the time both sides agree not to kill anyone who steps into the clearing. What are you doing here? I ordered all the women back to the carriages. It won't be safe here."

"Peace treaty," Anna Khordoa puffed, desperately trying to catch her breath. "War isn't needed. All done now. Stop — fighting."

"That's right, both sides have agreed to share the gold mine!" I agreed. "We're two seconds away from a peace treaty! Okay, I said that several minutes ago. But we're really close!"

"This is about far more than the gold," another red-capped man said tightly. "This is about victory."

"Then *both* sides can win!" I shouted.

Mocking laughter rang out from the bitter soldiers around me.

"The naivete of women," one of the men said shortly. "The war can't end without a winner. We have to *win*."

Anna Khordoa stared at him with narrowed eyes. Then she marched forward into the clearing, past the corpses, through the seemingly endless expanse of the ten feet in between the two forest patches.

The men around me looked uneasy. They exchanged looks at each other.

"I think she just went to be taken hostage," I said.

But a few minutes later, she was back, walking purposefully through the muck and the gore, not even seeming to notice it.

"Right," she said. "I'm renegotiating with their officers. I said they can have fifty-five percent of the gold mine, as long as they agree that we win. They said they're willing to take forty-five percent as long as *they* win."

"No!" one of the red-capped men spat. "They can have sixty percent, but we have to win!"

Anna Khordoa marched back across the filthy expanse. A few minutes later, she returned. "Guess what they said."

"Seventy percent, as long as we win!" several of the officers shouted, not waiting for her to repeat it.

She turned to head back across the clearing —

"Eighty percent!" a voice shouted from the other side.

"Ninety percent!" a voice shouted from our side.

"One hundred percent!" a voice shouted from their side.

"One hundred percent, and one of our iron mines!"

"One hundred percent, and two of our copper mines!"

"One hundred percent, and three of our iron mines!"

"One hundred percent, and four of our copper mines!"

"My mind is boggled," I muttered as Anna Khordoa walked back over, reaching my side. "How long do you think this can last?"

"Forever," she said, "or at least until both sides bargain away their entire kingdoms."

"That'll be interesting, having to call Horhold Gemina and Gemina Horhold," I said. "What'll the kings do?"

"Probably get bargained away along with everything else," Anna Khordoa said.

The numbers were still mounting in a frenzy.

"One hundred of our copper mines!"

"Two hundred of our iron mines!"

"Do we even *have* that many iron mines in Horhold?" I asked Anna Khordoa.

"No, we have four," she said. "And Gemina has three copper mines. Shh, don't stop them. I'm intrigued to see if they'll figure it out on their own."

"Two thousand of our copper mines!"

"Three thousand of our iron mines!"

"Offhand, I would say no," I said.

"Two million of our copper mines!"

"Three million of our iron mines!"

"I wonder how many numbers they know?" Anna Khordoa wondered.

"Not enough to make this last forever, which means we have to do something if we don't want them to break out fighting again," I said. I raised my mouth to a shout, and called, "How about Horhold wins because it conquers one of Gemina's copper mines, and Gemina wins because it conquers one of Horhold's iron mines?"

There was silence for a long moment.

"That might be possible!" a voice called from the other side.

"As long as we still get one hundred percent of the gold mine!" somebody from our side shouted.

"Ten percent!"

"Twenty percent!"

"Thirty percent!"

"Forty percent!"

"Fifty percent!"

"Fine, as long as we get the bigger half!"

Anna Khordoa threw up her hands.

"It's agreed!" I shouted. "The war is over! Everyone goes back home now!"

There were murmurs of confusion from both sides.

"And it was all because of me, Anna Khordoa, your child of prophecy!" Anna Khordoa hollered from beside me.

"What?" I exclaimed. "No, it wasn't! I—"

I paused. Why did I even want to win this argument?

"Okay, fine," I whispered. "You can be the child of prophecy."

"Don't act like you're being gracious," she hissed. "I *am* the child of prophecy."

"Look," I whispered, "it doesn't matter what *is*, remember? It only matters what *seems* to be. Just like Gemina and Horhold both have to believe they won so that the war won't seem completely pointless, even though it, in actual fact, was. If everyone believes you're the child of prophecy, whether or not you actually are, you will be."

Her face seemed to be deciding between mollified or offended.

"Try being mollified," I suggested.

"Fine," she whispered. "But you can't take it back!"

"Why would I want to?" I whispered back. "I never wanted to be a potential child of prophecy in the first place. I'm glad the burden's lifted from me."

She smiled smugly.

"Well, mostly glad," I added. "I still don't like you, and I wish it could have been the fortune teller who is not named Helga instead."

CHAPTER 20

TWENTY MORE SUGGESTIONS THAT ARE NOT WELL-RECEIVED

The king was not impressed by our solution to the problem.

"I said *victory!*" he shouted, pounding his fist on the goldwood throne.

"You really shouldn't pound like that," I added. "The right side is already lower than the left side. Have you done that before? Maybe you should pound the left side and both back sides instead if you don't want the throne to start leaning. You need to consider structural integrity when you pound things. Oh, you also left an almost-imperceptible dent."

"Really, Your Majesty," Anna Khordoa said coolly, "there was no way that the war was ever going to end unless both sides could claim they'd gotten what they wanted."

"Trust a woman!" the king shouted. "I should have known better than to trust any of you to have decent ideas! Now the past fifty years have been utterly *wasted!*" He slammed his fist down even harder.

"Now your throne is starting to tilt," I noted. "If you pound it again, it might collapse. Do you use smiths or carpenters to fix goldwood? I'm guessing carpenters, since goldwood is mildly flammable and you couldn't temper it like metal."

"The Fates are women, too," Anna Khordoa said, her eyes gleaming. "Is being a woman somehow an insult?"

The king hesitated. He didn't look like he wanted to answer.

Anna Khordoa waited silently, looking smug.

"I've insulted the Fates multiple times and had no consequences!" I interjected. "It's pretty great!"

There was a rumble outside.

"I mean, I've been adequately punished and learned my lesson and will never do it again," I added.

"Fine," King Derroll muttered, looking at Anna Khordoa. "There were much worse options to become the child of prophecy. From now on, you will remain in the castle to be educated in the ways of ruling." He hesitated. "As for my sons . . ."

"I believe an alliance with Gemina to cement our new peace would be in order, Your Majesty," Anna Khordoa said smoothly. "Their crown prince is unmarried."

"Ah," the king said, looking relieved. "Yes. Quite."

"I have a suggestion," I said. "I think you should keep Asaya here to educate her in the ways of not being an idiot. Also, the fortune teller should stay and educate the self-important charlatan. If you want, I'll look for someone who can educate your soothsayer, too."

The king looked at me in amazement. "Where do you find the gall to say such things? You realize you could be executed! Since you are not the child of prophecy, I can blame you for any mistakes that happened in the negotiations today. Do you not see that is why you're here?"

"That's pretty unsettling," I said. "I'd rather you not."

"Then don't anger me," he growled.

"Then don't talk to me," I retorted. "You're the one who started this conversation by making us come straight here instead of going back home. You have a lot of bigger problems to deal with than worrying about who to blame for any mistakes, anyway. Like the fact that all those soldiers will be coming back home. I suggest you turn most of the former soldiers into miners and send women out there who are *not* disreputable so that they can get married. If you don't, the city's population's going to get too high."

"I don't need —" the king began.

"That would also solve your second problem, which is that the city is getting way too crowded and we don't have nearly enough farmlands to support it, which is why there are so many kids on the streets going hungry," I said.

"I don't need your —" the king tried.

"You should offer any family who's lost a son in the war free farmland in thanks for his service," I said. "That'd mollify a lot of angry commoners and get them out of the city, which would break the power of the crime lords who are calling for revolution. If you don't think we have enough empty land to do that, there's a whole spot next to the border that's been doing nothing useful for fifty years."

"I don't —!"

"Who's been supplying the food to feed the soldiers in the first place?" I demanded. "Was it the disreputable women who they seemed used to having visit them?"

"They're not disreputable!" the king snapped. "The surrounding towns had immunity from the draft in exchange for —"

"Oh, good, then you can keep on taxing them that much and have them send it to the city instead," I said. "Then distribute it to the street urchins for free."

The king's face turned red. "I am not going to —"

"Next, you should do something to prevent the lingering resentment for Gemina that might flare up into another war in a generation," I said. "I suggest using the copper mine within their borders that is now ours to establish a community that interacts with their commoners on a regular basis. Probably you'd wind up with some intermarrying, which wouldn't be a bad thing. The iron mine within our borders that is now theirs could be used the same way —"

"Enough!" the king shouted, whamming the throne extra hard. "I do not need your advice! I do not want it! You are a commoner! You are a scapegoat! You are —"

The whole throne tilted to the side and collapsed. The king whammed on his head and rolled across the floor.

"Uncle!" Anna Khordoa gasped, running over to him.

"He's fine. He's breathing," I said. "I have twenty more suggestions. Do you want them now or later?"

The king picked himself up, his face red with fury or possibly humiliation.

"Go," he growled. "Get out of here. I want you out of my sight."

"I thought you wanted me to be a scapegoat," I said.

"If you don't want to be one, *go!*" He jabbed a finger out at the exit.

"Okay," I said. "If you want any more advice, you know where to find me. Actually, I don't want you to know where to find me. Don't have anyone follow me."

I marched to the door and threw it open. Then my way was blocked by several guards until the king came up behind me and informed them that I should be allowed to leave, which rather spoiled my exit. Still, I was soon marching down the market square, breathing in the fresh air of — actually, the air smelled like sour chicken droppings, but that was only because I was passing a stall filled with clucking cages. I passed it and breathed in the fresh air —

Nope, that was a cart selling manure.

I reached home and found Ma sitting outside, still weeping. My married sister Elayn was sitting beside her, patting her shoulder. They didn't even see me approach.

"Hi, the war is over and my brothers should be coming home now," I said. "The king hasn't made an official announcement, but you can spread rumors all you want. Of course, that is assuming he won't force the newly-drafted men and boys to work in the mine instead, but even if he does, it won't be as dangerous."

"Henina!" Ma gasped, looking up. "What is — what —?"

"What are you doing, giving her false hope like that?" Elayn asked furiously. "You never know when to shut your mouth or —"

"It's not false hope; the war is over," I said. "Really pretty simple once you got some people with sense out there. And twenty or so without it. I told the king he should give everyone who's lost a son in the war free farmland, which I probably shouldn't have told you because he said he wasn't going to do it, but if that starts a rumor and he then feels forced to do it, well, so much the better."

"You did it?" Ma whispered, looking up at me with red, blotchy eyes. "You're the child of prophecy?"

"No, that was Anna Khordoa," I said. "But it could have been worse. Another rumor you might want to start is that the king's going to give street urchins free food, especially if they throw rotten garbage at the castle until he starts."

"What are you talking about?!" Elayn exclaimed. "You're nuts!"

"Fine, I'll start the rumor myself," I said, exasperated. "Do I have to do everything?"

"Henina," Ma said unsteadily, "if what you're saying is true, then . . ."

A crowd was gathering around us, murmurs rising.

"Oh, yeah, Pa's three days behind in his work," I said. "Let me find something to work on while I'm spreading rumors. I can't wait to get things back to normal again. It's pretty great that I insulted the Fates, and there were no consequen . . ."

Light flashed out of the clear blue sky and stabbed our roof. People screamed, and I could scarcely hear them because my ears rang so badly from the tremendous noise. My eyes were blinking afterimages, pinkpurpleblueyellowgreen.

"Henina's bed just got struck by lightning!" Veiet screamed, bursting out of the house.

"What else caught fire?!" Ma gasped, leaping up.

"Nothing," Pa panted, jogging out of the house. "I have no clue how it's possible, but somehow only her bed — oh, hi, Henina —"

"It's okay," I said. "I'll just sleep on the floor instead."

Another bolt burst from the blue and struck our house again.

"Or the kitch—" I began.

"*No!*" Ma and Veiet and Elayn shouted.

"It s-seems clear," Pa stuttered, "that the Fates don't want you to live here anymore."

I stared at him blankly. "But I do live here. I don't have anywhere else to go."

"Did you say you insulted the Fates? That's why they did this!" one of our neighbors shouted at me. "We won't have you bringing your doom upon us all! Get out!"

"Get out! Get out! Get out!" the crowd began chanting.

I was speechless.

CHAPTER 21

TWENTY-ONE PUPPIES AND WISDOM AND GRACE

Since I had no clue what to do, I just wandered the streets aimlessly.

"I did everything I was supposed to," I complained to the Fates. "Why are you doing this to me? It's not like I mean to offend you. I just don't know how to keep my mouth shut."

There was no answer, not even a rumble.

I wandered into the marketplace, and people in the crowd began eyeing me nervously as I talked to myself.

"Come on," I muttered, looking up at the sky. "At least tell me if you're out to make me miserable or if you want something from me. Should I ask a fortune teller? I don't have any money on me, though. Oh, wait, I have the gold ore, but I'd need to find a smelter who won't ask any questions to buy it from me, and I'm not sure where to . . ."

"You!" a voice shouted.

I looked up and saw the king's guard who had taken the draft dodge money pointing at me. He was holding an apple in his other hand.

"You!" I shouted back, pointing at him because it seemed like something to do. "What do you want? I don't know your name."

"The king wants you," the guard said darkly, lifting the apple up to his mouth to take a bite.

"That's a quarter-iron!" the woman at the stall beside him snapped, reaching out to snatch it from him. "Pay first, eat later!"

The guard stared at her for a moment, looking taken aback. He fumbled in his pockets to find a thin iron coin, then carefully bent it backwards down the middle until it snapped. He snapped one of the halves in half again and handed it to the woman.

"Well, bye," I said, starting to walk off.

"Wait!" the guard called. "Stop! The king wants you!"

"The king let me go," I said. "Your information's out of date."

"It is not!" the guard shouted. "He sent four of us out to look for you ten minutes ago!"

I turned around and stared at him. "Why?"

"I don't know," he said, waving his hands. "He just said —"

My stomach growled. "Okay, buy me an apple and I'll go back with you."

"Apples are a half-iron," the woman beside him said helpfully.

"They were a quarter-iron a second ago!" he protested.

"You misheard. They're three quarter-irons."

"I'm not buying an apple at that price!" he fumed.

I shrugged and turned to go.

"Wait!" the guard shouted, fumbling in his pocket for the sections of coin he'd dropped in there. "Okay, okay! Here!"

A very happy apple seller pocketed her money while I bit into my apple. It was mushy and a little soggy, but better than nothing.

I followed the guard back to the castle while I chewed and swallowed, scraping out the seeds with my teeth. I finished the last of the core, tucked the seeds and the stem in my pocket, and licked the juice off my fingers. My stomach was still growling as we reached the throne room.

The king wasn't there, so the guard sent for a servant to fetch him. While he was doing that, I wandered over to the sagging throne and kicked it. That left a noticeable dent.

"What are you doing?" the guard asked, sounding weary.

"Checking to see how much of a nightmare this will be to fix," I said. "I'm glad I'm not in charge of it. Unless I am. Is that why the king wants to see me?"

"I have no idea," the guard said. "I have no idea why anyone would want you around on purpose."

"Then you don't have much imagination," I said.

The king arrived, walking briskly and flourishing a fur-lined cape behind him.

"You weren't wearing that before," I said. "It looks hot and stifling."

"It occurs to me," the king said formally, "that I do not have an advisor."

"That's right," I agreed. "There hasn't been one since your father cut off the last one's head."

"I want you to take the position."

"No," I said. "I like my head where it is."

"In that case," he said, eyebrows twitching, "take the position!"

"Why do you think threatening me would result in good advice?"

King Derroll's jaw clenched.

"Well, if that's it, I'll be going," I said.

"What else do you want?" he snapped. "Is it money? Gold? Jewels?"

"Yes," I said immediately. "All of those. How much are you offering?"

His eyebrows twitched. "That is contingent on how much of a difference your advice makes to the finances of the country."

"Does it come with a place to live?" I asked.

"A place can be found in the servants' quarters —"

"No, I want a nice room, like Anna Khordoa's," I said. "And really nice food. And my brothers to come back to the city, unless they'd rather work in the mine. Oh, and I want a dog. Mainly because that's the next thing that came to mind, but also because only rich people can afford pets, and I want to feel rich."

"Anything else?" the king asked tightly.

"Probably. Why did you change your mind about listening to me?"

The king said nothing for a long moment.

"If you think out loud, it works better," I said helpfully. "I dunno why more people don't do it."

"I think," the king said slowly, "that your manner is annoying, but your insights are impressive, and that wisdom may be something that Horhold needs."

"I agree," I said. "On all counts."

He paused. "You agree that your manner is annoying?"

I shrugged. "It's not like I'm unaware, it's just that I've accepted there's not much that I can do about it."

"You could *try*," he said.

"Eh, that's brainpower I can put to much better use," I said, waving my hand. "You've just validated that."

The king's eyebrows twitched.

The door behind the king opened, and a harassed-looking woman in shredded clothes stormed in, carrying a growling brown-furred puppy. "Your Majesty, we need to get rid of this one. It won't stop destroying everything. It won't be trained. It'll never be useful for hunting. I've trained twenty-one puppies in the last year, but this one is . . ."

"Oh, that's my dog!" I said promptly, running over. "Hi, pretty brown puppy! Are you a boy or a girl? What's your name?"

The dog snapped at my fingers.

"If you want it, take it," the woman said wearily. "We've been calling her Grace."

I stared at the woman in horror as the dog tried to bite me again. She'd arrived right after I'd said I wanted a dog, which was a coincidence. I'd thought I was safe, but no, my life was still being manipulated.

"The Fates are keeping their options open, just in case Anna Khordoa doesn't work out," I muttered under my breath. "Being the king's advisor could count as ruling, he just said I had wisdom, and they knew they couldn't possibly give me grace . . ."

"You definitely don't want this one," the woman said, nodding. "I'll have it slaughtered."

"No, I'll take the dog!" I exclaimed. "How could you even say that? Give her to me!"

I grabbed the vicious puppy, which tried to bite my elbow, and I held her away from my face as she wriggled and snarled.

"Your name is now Mud," I declared.

ABOUT THE AUTHOR

Emily Martha Sorensen doesn't have a penchant for annoying people, but she does like to talk a lot. She was given the "Most Likely to Bite Off Tongue While Talking" award at her high school graduation. The best way to keep her quiet is to give her a good book, unless the book is funny: then she'll probably laugh out loud.

She writes young adult, middle grade, and clean new adult fantasy.